PAST
TITAN
ROCK

PAST
TITAN
ROCK

JOURNEYS INTO AN
APPALACHIAN
VALLEY

ELLESA CLAY HIGH

THE UNIVERSITY PRESS OF KENTUCKY

Published by the University Press of Kentucky:
Scholarly publisher for the Commonwealth,
serving Bellarmine College, Berea College, Centre
College of Kentucky, Eastern Kentucky University,
The Filson Club, Georgetown College, Kentucky
Historical Society, Kentucky State University,
Morehead State University, Murray State University,
Northern Kentucky University, Transylvania University,
University of Kentucky, University of Louisville,
and Western Kentucky University.
Editorial and Sales Offices: Lexington, Kentucky 40506-0024

Library of Congress Cataloging in Publication Data

High, Ellesa Clay, 1948-
  Past Titan Rock.

  1. Red River Gorge (Ky.)—Social life and customs.
2. Red River Valley (Ky.)—Social life and customs.
3. Red River Gorge (Ky.)—Biography. 4. Red River Valley
(Ky.)—Biography. 5. Red River Gorge (Ky.)—Fiction.
6. Red River Valley (Ky.)—Fiction. I. Title.
F457.R4H54 1984   306'.09769'76   83-23387
ISBN 0-8131-1505-1

CONTENTS

In memory of Dave Maurer

ACKNOWLEDGMENTS

I'm grateful to the many people who helped in producing this book, only a few of whom are mentioned here. I'm indebted to Professors Jack Matthews, Gere Krebs, Robert Roe, and Mark Rollins of Ohio University for their many readings and criticisms of the manuscript during much of its writing. Also I would like to thank Mr. Larry G. Meadows, President of the Red River Historical Society and Museum, for sharing his knowledge and many years of experience in the field, and Ms. Karen Conrad, a Louisville attorney, for her assistance with research in legal history. A special appreciation goes to Professor Leon Driskell of the University of Louisville, who introduced me to Lily May Ledford and encouraged my initial writing concerning her, and to Loyal Jones, Director of the Appalachian Center at Berea College, for his continued assistance and interest in my work concerning the Appalachian region. Certainly, I would like to thank my family, especially my parents, and close friends for their personal support. And for their clerical assistance with this manuscript, I would like to thank the secretarial staff of the English Department at West Virginia University.

Finally, I want to thank all my friends in the Red River Gorge. Without their generosity, honesty, and warmth, this book would have been impossible to complete or even to begin. No words of appreciation can express my gratitude to Lily May Ledford for her invaluable assistance of five years, or to the farmer and his family who so kindly lent me a place to live on the river.

Portions of the oral history with Lily May Ledford have appeared in a different form in *Adena: A Journal of the History and Culture of the Ohio River Valley* and *The Courier-Journal Magazine*. The short story, "Pigeon Milk," was published in the anthology, *Step Around the Mountain*.

INTRODUCTION

There are no whole truths; all truths are
half-truths. It is trying to treat them
as whole truths that plays the devil.

ALFRED NORTH WHITEHEAD

To experience the Red River Gorge in the mountains of eastern Kentucky, you might hike to Indian Staircase. Take the Sheltowee Trace which climbs the ridge nearby, or follow Sargent Branch of Gladie Creek and scramble up the worn Adena cuts in the cliff. At the head of a box canyon jammed with sugar maples, wahoos, and myriad other trees, you'll find a rock house or cave opening of impressive size. It will be quiet, except for a thin spring which jumps and glitters from the top ledge. The zigzag trail of snakes will lie silent too in the dust. During the week, you can camp there undisturbed.

Or if you are in a hurry, drive to Sky Bridge, the largest and most popular arch of the seventy or more dotting the Gorge. It will not be quiet and you will not be alone, at least if the tour buses are discharging their crowds in the parking lot. Follow the signs and sidewalk; you can't miss it. As you tread the sandstone, initial-riddled back of the arch, which reaches broad and heavy as a dinosaur neck in stone, you may also be impressed.

But then try to find the Bluefield or Old Monkeyface, the Boardtree Holler or Lysh Brown Cliff. You will be going places not marked on the maps you've counted upon. These also are part of the Red River Gorge, but to get to them you need a human guide and you must travel into the past. Then you'll discover the way, though this trail may not start in the Gorge itself.

For me it began ninety miles to the west in a small town in central Kentucky.

The evening draped itself heavy, hot, and clear over the fields and the town, which was celebrating a homecoming fair. Friends and relatives had gathered for the weekend, many returning to a community quite changed from their last visit. These days the village is home for two disparate groups: the farmers and small merchants whose families have lived there for generations, and an influx of young people, many of them artists, craftspersons, and others attempting to "return to the land." The latter tend to be college-educated, liberal, socially eclectic, and willing to subsist hand-to-mouth in order

to practice their vocations full time. While each group appreci-
ates certain qualities of the other, both coexist with some
tension and mistrust.

This night, however, many were crowded into a house not
far from town to celebrate the anniversary of a local farmer.
Most appeared cheerful, almost boisterous, as they snacked on
pickled beans and corn, fresh tomatoes, zucchini bread, pies
of apple and cushaw, home-slaughtered and home-cured
ham, and fried chicken. Friends and neighbors milled through
the kitchen and spilled onto the porch. I had been invited by a
printer, who was related to the young farmer's wife.

At an unseen signal, instruments were pulled from closets
and corners; the entertainment was to be home-grown as well.
As several men unsnapped their cases and began tuning, it
seemed that music connected these people as much as blood
ties, friendships, or the proximity of neighbors. The musicians
inspected each other's instruments, joked, and offered a tenta-
tive song. The rest of the guests clapped and sang, then one by
one returned to conversation. Occasionally pausing to sip their
beers, the musicians drew closer together and played through
a string of tunes.

Then a woman at least six feet tall stepped through the
front door. Though gray haired, smiling and soft spoken, she
radiated that quality which causes a roomful of people to turn
and stare. The music stopped. With much handshaking, the
players ushered her into their circle, and a stocky, gallused
man bashfully thrust his fiddle toward her.

She plucked the strings, complimented him, then propped
the violin on her chest rather than tucking it under her chin.
Wielding the bow with great energy, she struck up "Sourwood
Mountain." Clapping resumed, only louder, and the plank
floor thumped and shook underfoot. Soon everyone was dancing and elbowing into each other. By midnight she had played
the bass fiddle, mandolin, guitar, and returned to home
ground on the fiddle and banjo. The most accomplished
performer there, she was also the only woman to touch an
instrument.

By one o'clock I was jigged and shouted out. As I walked to my car, vague lantern light scattering the dark, her music followed me merry and strong, and apparently unstoppable.

While I was wandering through the community fair the next afternoon, an editor I knew from Louisville approached me. Would I write an article for his journal? he asked. He wanted an oral history interview with an old-time musician from the Red River Gorge. Lily May Ledford had led the Coon Creek Girls, a group generally considered the first all-girl string band on radio back in the 1930s, and her accomplishments reflected pioneering efforts in a field where few women previously had been successful. As he talked, I guessed that she was the woman I'd seen the night before.

I wasn't well acquainted with old-time music, though I'd heard snatches of it all my life, and I knew nothing about early radio days. But I thought I knew the Gorge, which is located in parts of Powell, Menifee, and Wolfe counties. I'd enjoyed camping there, and hiking its major trails. And I'd been born and raised in Kentucky, so I understood something about the people. Then there was the woman herself. Both she and the idea for the article intrigued me. I hesitated, then accepted, adding that I would need a few weeks to "prepare."

How little did I understand what preparation would entail in this instance, for it was five months before I was ready to attempt the interview. I had read everything I could find on country music and its roots, and my editor suggested scholars and musicians who could tell me more about old-time, traditional groups, particularly those from the eastern mountains. Their support had been encouraging and generous. By January I felt I could ask questions and respond without seeming hopelessly ignorant.

The interview lasted most of the day, and Lily May's radio career proved as engaging as I had anticipated. But even more fascinating were her reminiscences of the Red River Gorge. She described a culture I had never known existed, one as colorful as the area's place names: Chimney Top, and Pinch-Em Tight, and the Calaboose. Each name sparked a story and the recollection of mountain life. I began to realize that while I had become familiar with the Gorge, it was not the one she knew.

The Gorge I knew had few people. Much of it had been purchased by the federal government in the 1930s and made part of the Daniel Boone National Forest. That forest today sprawls over half a million acres of Kentucky, including the Red River Gorge, a serpentine puzzle of ridges, cliffs, white water, and stone arches. But despite the grandeur of its trees and overlooks, in reality it is a cutover remnant of one of the greatest hardwood forests on earth, which until this century covered much of the eastern United States. For example, in the 1880s a band mill on Red River was considered the second largest of its kind in the world, and at its busiest produced over 200,000 board feet per day.[1] And the Gorge continued to supply lumber on a similar scale for years. This and related activities attracted people who could survive by their wits and by herculean labor in a land that was exacting, dense, and mysterious. These loggers and rivermen, hunters, fishers and trappers, boatmakers, railroaders and blasters, the few large farmers, and an accompanying stream of sharecroppers all depended upon resources they were depleting at a ferocious rate.

When the logging companies finished and the railroads closed down, many families had no choice but to leave. Few, aside from the sprinkling of established settlers who owned the narrow bottomlands of the river, could support themselves. This exodus, later accelerated by government purchases, the Great Depression, and the general migration of Appalachians to northern cities during the 1940s through the 1960s, emptied the Gorge of most of its population. Today the forest has grown back to proportions impressive to visitors who have not glimpsed old photographs of tree trunks so thick they required six-foot, crosscut saws to fell them. In contrast, however, the departed people of Red River have not returned. Their hills now are federal property, and jobs in the area are still scarce.

On that freezing day of January 5, 1977, I listened to Lily

May recall a time and a culture rich with music, custom, folklore, and oral tradition, and I felt we would have to talk again. I was right. Our conversations would spread over four years, and we would travel the Gorge together as well. I would be introduced to those who still live on the fringes of the forest, clinging fiercely to their ancestral homes and beliefs. Others I would trace to nursing homes and distant towns. I would seek out their cabins, trailers, and new brick split-levels, spend hours with families on their porches, and accompany them through their tobacco barns and graveyards. Sometimes I was turned away. More often I was taken in like an old friend. Occasionally I was given very personal information with the trust usually reserved for kin. And for months I would live by myself in the Gorge, trying to understand as intimately as possible a place and a way of life I had not experienced before. Gradually I learned about a culture almost gone, existing mostly in memory, in song, and in the names of places whose human history had disappeared as completely as their gigantic trees.

Kentucky writer Jim Wayne Miller has pointed out Appalachia's need for meaningful links with its past. When written records have been scantily kept, however, establishing such connections becomes especially difficult. As critic John Berger has said, "The past is never there waiting to be discovered, to be recognized for exactly what it is."[2] Both objective facts and our consciousness of those facts must be considered.

To date, little has been written concerning the people of Red River or the rich culture that thrived there. Yet well over a hundred thousand visitors annually are attracted to its ridges.[3] The majority of tourists, most of whom have driven from nearby Lexington, Louisville, and Cincinnati, never leave the main road looping the Gorge. Many never step out of their cars. Few of those who backpack into the hollows or canoe the river care to meet the local residents: they are trying to escape people, not meet them. It's the Appalachian hills they want.

Despite the Gorge's inclusion in the Wild and Scenic Rivers Program, the Wilderness Area Program, and the National

Landmark Program, as well as its listing in the National Register of Historic Places and as a Forest Service Special Interest Area, much of its culture has gone unstudied.[4] In a sense, this fits a pattern often noted about Appalachian culture in general. Until recently, the people of central Appalachia have produced comparatively little of the literature concerning their region, and all too often they have been either ignored, exploited, caricatured, or idealized by scholars, writers, and others from the dominant culture, or the "outside world," as Jack Weller has called it.[5]

Beginning this book, I questioned how I, not being native to the mountains, could avoid stereotyping the people of Red River and their past. One strategy has been to write from several viewpoints, both in content and form. For instance, by varying style and approach, I hoped to minimize assumptions of language or cultural distortions. Also, I was interested in examining through first-hand use some of the distinctions between genres, particularly since such hybrids as the prose poem, the docu-drama, and "fact-fiction" seem to signal a change in our traditional classifications of literature, and to question our conventional interpretation of "fact" itself.

Edward Abbey has observed that "there is a kind of poetry, even a kind of truth in simple fact."[6] His work, as well as that by such other prose stylists as Wendell Berry and John McPhee, illustrates that nonfiction is useful for more than the presentation of objective fact. For example, in *Desert Solitaire* Abbey explores the history, geography, ecology, and other aspects of the Arches region in Utah. By occasionally using techniques more often found in fiction, however, he portrays the desert in a stylistically vivid manner. Through his impressions we come to know the taste, sound, and texture of this landscape; and when he imagines the thoughts, motivations, and actions of people long dead, he brings the past alive in a way more scholarly studies cannot. What he offers may not be objective in the customary sense, but it can be as revealing a look at an area as we may find.

In Part One of this book I have tried to present the Gorge and its people in a similar fashion. This includes my personal observations, as well as information concerning local history, folklore, and beliefs, among other subjects. While "Past Titan Rock" looks briefly at topics which deserve more detailed study, I agree with Abbey when he reflects in *Desert Solitaire*, "Language makes a mighty loose net with which to go fishing for simple facts, when facts are infinite. If a man knew enough he could write a whole book about the juniper tree." And, with reference to his own project, he states: "Not imitation but evocation has been the goal" (p. x).

Part Two, "A View from Chimney Top," attempts to create a sense of Red River as it was earlier in this century, through a witnessing of that time and place. Oral history is particularly effective for recording the way of life of those who have relied on spoken rather than written traditions, or those who have felt alienated from the dominant culture. It lessens the likelihood of stereotyped treatment by going straight to the people and in effect saying, *What you have to tell about your experience is of value, not only to yourself but to others.* This message is one that Appalachian people have heard too rarely. Ohio writer Jack Matthews has observed, "Today, the art of the story teller is that of a socially acceptable lie."[7] For the central Appalachian, it is a means of communicating the socially unacceptable truth as well.

Although I've given priority to preserving Lily May's personal voice and her authentic account of mountain life, I've also tried to reproduce her story as succinctly as possible. By this I mean that I chose material from hours of interviewing that were taped over several years and reconstructed from written notes. I deleted my questions and repetitious language, then edited the text into a single setting and narration. I did not, however, homogenize character; Lily May's words and insights remain her own.[8]

Because of its style and her choice of role, Lily May's story approximates what folklorist Richard Dorson has defined as the "personal saga": "The teller of personal sagas is a master narrator who portrays himself as a hero derring-do in bold adventures or a sad-sack in bumbling misadventures that take on mythic outlines, through what appear to be frequent retellings. He creates his own legend."[9] Given that Lily May displays these characteristics, it's not surprising that a monograph summarizing her musical career was titled, *Lily May Ledford: A Legend in Our Time* (by Kenneth Hull, New York: Carlton Press, 1970). She possesses a keen memory, the knack for relating vivid details, and a discerning humor. She also takes obvious pleasure in entertaining an audience. Her story is romantic, yet episodic and expressed in plain language.

These characteristics add a picaresque quality to her account. As she relates how her sharecropper family drifted through the Gorge, she pictures herself as having overcome the obstacles of backwoods poverty through ingenuity, perseverance, and luck. While sometimes assuming the role of the passive mountaineer, she nevertheless implies that she often outwitted authority, and she describes in an innocent and amusing manner how she managed to skirt the traditional behavior then expected of mountain women.

Material concerning Lily May's life after she left the Gorge and her long career as a professional musician has been included in an epilogue. Her remembrances of early radio days, her impressions of performing on WLS's "National Barn Dance" and of playing at the White House before the king and queen of England, and her anecdotes concerning Woodie Guthrie, Red Foley, and other performers may be noteworthy to those interested in the history of country and old-time music.

The third and final part of this book consists of a cycle of short stories set in the Gorge. Here, however, Red River is a starting point; and what I heard and learned by living there has been dramatically reshaped. For example, in "The Luck of Elmer White," the plot centers around the building of the Nada Tunnel, and the description of its construction is based directly on oral accounts given to me by two of the few survivors of those who worked on the tunnel around 1911. The main character, however, is partially imagined and partially a mixture of persons I've met during different periods in my life, for facts need not confine the fiction writer. I borrowed the name "Furnace Mountain" from an actual ridge, but it is one that lies some ten or fifteen miles west of the Gorge. The "East Fork" of Red River, where the community of Furnace Mountain is located in the stories, does not exist.

By taking a fictional approach I've included material from a variety of sources, as well as my own imagination, in a way impossible in oral history without sacrificing authenticity. Tape transcriptions rarely make good fictional dialogue, nor do written words "hear right" as oral history. In addition, material we might misinterpret if presented as straight oral history may be defined more clearly for us in fiction or in other types of nonfiction prose.

Writing about the Gorge and its people from fictional and nonfictional perspectives is similar to photographing it with both color and black-and-white film. While we may have a preference for one, neither is intrinsically superior to the other if handled with equal care and vision. We don't judge a black-and-white picture as a failure if it isn't charged with blue. Likewise, each writing form offers unique advantages. By freely using several or combining them in different relationships, we have a chance to create fresh aesthetic effects.

Wendell Berry has commented in *The Unforeseen Wilderness*, his book on the Red River Gorge created in collaboration with the photographer, Ralph Eugene Meatyard:

> The camera is a point of reference, a bit like a compass though not nearly so predictable. It is the discipline and opportunity of vision. In relation to the enclosure we call civilization, these pictures are not ornaments or relics, but windows and doors, enlargements of our living space, entrances into the mysterious world outside the walls, lessons in what to look for and how to see. They limit our comfort; they drain away the subtle corruption of being smug; they make us a little afraid, for they suggest always the presence of the unknown, what lies outside the picture and beyond eyesight . . . they can serve as spiritual landmarks in the pilgrimage to the earth that each one of us must take alone. (pp. 33–34)

Whether our point of reference be fiction, nonfiction, or some hybrid form, each can help provide meaningful links to the past, and if we're lucky, links between ourselves and other people.

Notes

1. Robert H. Ruchhoft, *Kentucky's Land of the Arches* (Cincinnati: Pucelle Press, 1976), p. 24.

2. John Berger, *Ways of Seeing* (New York: British Broadcasting Corporation and Penguin Books, 1972), p. 11.

3. This figure is quite conservative. Other sources indicate an annual visitor rate between 300,000–500,000, a number which seemed to peak in the mid-1970s after the Gorge had received national media coverage concerning a controversial dam project proposed for the area. By combining attendance of the Gorge and nearby Natural Bridge State Park, Ruchhoft (1976) estimates a visitor rate of almost one million per year.

4. The publications which have appeared concerning the Gorge include trail guides, a few privately printed monographs on certain historical events or industries, a fine reproduction of a "photograph album" of scenes around Natural Bridge State Park, a study of fishes in the Red River drainage, and some material concerning the legend of John Swift's silver mine. Ruchhoft's guide, *Kentucky's Land of the Arches*, is one of the most helpful publications to appear concerning the Gorge. A historian, he quickly surveys the history of the area before describing the major trails. Other individuals, working within the U.S. Forest Service, and those who created and maintain the Red River Historical Museum, have for many years shown keen interest in collecting and preserving the cultural heritage of the Gorge.

The most striking publication, however, is *The Unforeseen Wilderness*, a volume written by Wendell Berry and accompanied by the photographs of Gene Meatyard (Lexington: University Press of Kentucky, 1971). Now out of print, this set of essays appeared at a crucial period when the U.S. Army Corps of Engineers had initiated plans for a dam which would have flooded much of the Gorge. A beautiful, contemplative book, it examines man's relationship to the earth, and his use and misuse of wilderness. However, though Berry often describes the Gorge in evocative detail, he seems mostly interested in more general questions: "I might as well leave the place anonymous, for what I have learned here could be learned from any woods and from any free-running river" (p. 94).

5. The reasons behind this stereotyping and underlying cultural differences are complex and embedded historically in the central and southern Appalachian experience. For more information concerning the general background of the region, the ethnic groups that settled there, their motivations for migration, and their subsequent history in America, the reader might consult these standard works in the field: John C. Campbell, *The Southern High-*

lander and His Homeland (New York: Russell Sage Foundation, 1921; rpt. Lexington: University Press of Kentucky, 1969, c1921); Harry M. Caudill, *Night Comes to the Cumberlands* (Boston: Little, Brown & Co., 1962); Robert J. Higgs and Ambrose M. Manning, eds., *Voices from the Hills: Selected Readings of Southern Appalachia* (New York: Frederick Ungar, 1975); James G. Leyburn, *The Scotch-Irish: A Social History* (Chapel Hill: University of North Carolina Press, 1962); Jack Weller, *Yesterday's People* (Lexington: University of Kentucky Press, 1965); Thomas Jefferson Wertenbaker, *The Old South: The Founding of American Civilization* (New York: Charles Scribner's Sons, 1942).

6. Edward Abbey, *Desert Solitaire* (New York: McGraw-Hill Book Company, 1968), p. xii.

7. Jack Matthews, *Tales of the Ohio Land* (Columbus: Ohio Historical Society, 1978), p. viii.

8. During the many times Lily May and I have visited and worked together, three taping sessions were particularly important:

a) January 5, 1977. This session lasted most of a day and produced approximately three hours of taped interviews. Material from these tapes was published a few months later as "The Coon Creek Girl from the Red River Gorge: An Interview with Lily May Pennington" (*Adena*, Spring 1977, pp. 44–74).

b) July 3–10, 1978. During this week, another dozen hours of tape were recorded. Some of these conversations included Lily May's brother, Coyen, who was visiting for the summer.

c) July 24, 1979. This session was recorded with the assistance of Ed McDonald, then a producer for radio station WOUB of the Telecommunications Center at Ohio University. With funding from the Satellite Program Development Fund of National Public Radio, material from these tapes was used to create an hour-long documentary, "Lily May Ledford: Banjo Pickin' Girl." Produced by McDonald, and written and narrated by the author, this program was distributed nationally via satellite in summer, 1982. Another half-hour version, "The Life and Music of Lily May Ledford," was completed by McDonald and High as a feature for National Public Radio's "Horizons" series during December, 1982.

Tapes from these and other sessions were transcribed into approximately one hundred pages of manuscript. During the editing process, this manuscript, in various stages of completion, was read by Lily May. Her comments and corrections not only eliminated many mistakes, but supplied supplemental material, which often led to more detailed discussions, further recording, and note taking.

9. Richard Dorson, *Folklore and Fakelore* (Cambridge: Harvard University Press, 1976), p. 140.

PART ONE

PAST
TITAN
ROCK

. . . go freely with powerful uneducated persons
and with the young and with the mothers of
families, read these leaves in the open air
every season of every year of your life, re-
examine all you have been told at school or
church or in any book, dismiss whatever insults
your own soul, and your very flesh shall be a
great poem and have the richest fluency not only
in its words but in the silent lines of its lips
and face and between the lashes of your eyes and
in every motion and joint of your body.

WALT WHITMAN

June 14, 1979

Time depends on the river here. To go where I want in the Gorge usually doesn't take long in the bone white heat of summer. You follow the asphalt highway through part of the Gorge, then veer onto a graveled, one lane road with passing places. If you know where to look, after a while you'll see a wash with tire tracks leading between two corn fields. When it's dry, you can skid down this gulley to a ford in the river. Once across, you're on the farm I'm aiming for, and it's only a few minutes before you pull up next to the yard.

But this summer has begun as the wettest on record, and the river is in no mood to be driven through. Its currents are quarrelling with its banks, the banks rank and feisty in return. So Red River is named after mud, I think, watching the clay-thick water sweep by. I don't dare try it. Though my Volkswagen bus sits high off the ground, today it's loaded with supplies. My dog, a black-and-white Llewellyn setter, is pacing the middle seat, tired of being cooped up. If I could just use what's left of this old country road which passes through the farm and beyond it, my trip would be finished. I look once more at the far bank, less than twenty feet away, and wonder how long it will take me to reach the other side.

Using high weeds for traction, I turn back on the gravel road and swing past the farmer's other house, the convenient one where he lives. He's not home. My only guide will be the instructions in his letter. I anxiously check them and the sky. Much of the afternoon is gone, and the sun doesn't linger in the hollows. I stay on this road until it crosses the river at Bowen, then head east, passing through the next jumble of houses called Nada, and up Snakey Holler to Nada Tunnel. Driving through the tunnel is like being swallowed whole by the mountain, with barely enough room to squeeze through. Cars at the other end, seven hundred feet away, must wait or back up. But today I'm alone in this unlit passage. I flash on my headlights and the mountain crowds in, its jagged sides playing tricks with my eyes. The ceiling seeps water and seems barely high enough for a van like mine.

Originally built for a standard gauge railroad, the tunnel

was constructed some seventy years ago by logging companies
eager to reach the vast forest in the lower half of the Gorge.
This signalled a boom period for the area, opening jobs for
loggers, blasters, railroaders, mechanics—virtually anyone
willing to work for twelve or more hours a day. As the railroad
grades and tracks were laid and the forest cut, shanties and
log houses cluttered the new clearings and relatively prosperous times prevailed until the logging operations were finished.
Then the tracks were removed, though the tunnel remained
open to foot and wagon traffic. I remember once hearing a
man say that he had driven through the tunnel with fireflies
for lights and mud up to his team's knees. Aside from asphalt
replacing the mud, little else has changed in the tunnel,
conditions which excite tourists and create traffic jams on
weekends.

I've got a feeling I won't have to worry about traffic where
I'm going. I pass Titan Rock, a hulk of stone jutting from a
ridge like the prow of a ship, and take what I hope is the right
turnoff. This narrow road climbs a ridge so steep my van
barely tops it in first gear. Then I'm in part of the Gorge I've
never visited before. The road descends close by the river, its
asphalt crumbling to gravel. In a mile or two it shrinks to a dirt
path bristling with rocks and pocked with mud holes. I stop
and recheck my instructions. I haven't seen a house in quite a
while, but this must be right. I creep forward again, slow
enough not to rip the car bottom on rocks, though I hope fast
enough not to get stuck in the mud. Anyway, that is my
strategy.

Now it's the forest that squeezes close, branches slapping
my windshield. If there were a place to turn around, I would,
but there is none. The road is dangling on a ridgeside which
drops some fifteen or twenty feet to the river. Just in front I see
a slippage. There is still space to pass, I judge, though no room
for error. Despite the slick mud, I decide to try it. Crossing
over, I glance down. Toward the bottom a car lies half-buried,
half-pillowed in the slide. Corroded and crumpled, it looks as if
it's been there for a long time, but who can tell.

All now is trees, or the shadows of trees. And mud and

gloom. I'm sure I've made a terrible mistake, and one I can't back out of. The trees thin, and up ahead the road looks blocked by a massive cliff. This miserable path must dead-end there, and I name the place "Face to the Wall." Finally, I see where the road eases past to the left. I follow, and the land spreads out again. I drive through an open gate and over a cattle guard. A hay field extends to one side and around one more curve a barn and house swing into view. As I stop by the yard fence, a big, fleshy man pushes to his feet from the front porch steps. It's the farmer. I open the car door, hot and relieved, and my dog jumps out to explore the new territory.

The farmer walks toward the gate, a deliberate, slow smile on his face. He says, "I just about gave up on you. What took you so long?" And he chuckles, because he knows. This man I've quickly met twice and not seen for a year, but he nevertheless will generously let me use his tenant house on the far side of his property. I can see that already I amuse him, provide a pleasant interruption to his routine—one reason I imagine he's letting me stay. Another is as a favor to Lily May Ledford, an old friend of his and of many people still living in and around the Gorge. Without her introduction, I wouldn't be here.

He shows me around the yard. It is neat and uncluttered. The grass has been freshly mowed, some weeds giving off a strange skunky smell. The house looks well cared for on the outside, its wood protected by clean white paint. He points out the well and nods toward the privy, which totters on the hillside beyond the fence. Then his eyes return to me, slow and brown as molasses, yet sharp. I doubt that he misses much. He says, "This house has been empty for seventeen years. Sometimes people get back in here that got no business poking around. I figure it wouldn't hurt having somebody watch the place for the summer." He pauses. "If you think you can handle that," he adds, chuckling again.

I assure him that I'll manage.

"That's good. That's real good," he says.

Waiting for me, he has unnailed the windows and reconnected the electricity. Now he helps me unload the van. We work quickly and without much talk, because night is fast approaching and a drizzle has started sifting through the tulip poplars by the house. Then he hands me the key and takes his leave, saying he will stop by sometime during the next week when he checks his cattle again. For him, the trip home is easy—a fifteen minute walk and a short boat ride. That's the way to travel in this part of the Gorge.

After a few minutes' rest, I inspect the inside of the house. For the Gorge, especially way back here, it's a fine place: electricity, a refrigerator and stove, no running water but a sweet, clear well. The three large rooms form an L-shape and include a kitchen, living room, and bedroom. Each has three doors—one connecting and two outside. Eight doors for a three-room house. I imagine the Marx Brothers dashing from one to another in time with crazy music. For a house more than a hundred years old, it looks reasonably strong. But there are spongy places in the floor, and the chimney, part field stone and part brick, is crumbling down. A yellow jacket nest plugs it closed. A coal stove in the living room, thin with rust, has been vented through the fireplace. Several stuffed chairs, a cedar wardrobe, an old sewing machine, and five tables fill up space. The gray linoleum on the kitchen floor and the sagging flowered cloth on a sofa have patterns similar to those I remember in my grandmother's house.

I feel as if I've come home. I know this furniture, this yard, the way the farmer laughed and lent a hand while silently evaluating me. Yes, I've been here before. And yet, I haven't. No one has lived here for years. The cover of a *Life* magazine is dated 1962. Dust furs the table tops, which are also peppered with what looks like seventeen years of mouse droppings. No drawer, no cranny I check is free from them.

I feed my dog, then open some chicken soup and eat it cold from the can. It tastes greasy and tinny, but I'm too tired to be very hungry. Besides, there's too much cleaning to do here before I can cook. A mouse pops from a hole in the floor, where seconds later a thin, periscope shape glides up. By the time I realize it's a snake, it has flashed me a frozen, incredulous look and disappeared. The only sound now is the flick of gnats swarming around the overhead light. There are just too many cracks in this house for screens to matter much. Switching off lights as I go, I lock the doors. Outside, the drizzle has stopped. In the bedroom, I shake mouse droppings off the old featherbed and watch them scatter like rice on the wooden floor. I spread my sleeping bag on top of the mattress and stretch out, and the smell of mold and old feathers covers me over. From the wall next to my head hangs a congregation of wasps, resting on a nest as big as a grapefruit. They, too, have settled in for the night.

July 17, 1979

Dawn breaks over the mountains, for a few seconds throwing a slab of light between cloud bank and earth. Then the ridges blur from sight. Rain comes across the valley, rippling dark olive in the trees and clattering against the tin roof of the house. The air thickens, and the whole place seems buried under water. This is a morning for doorways, for standing in between, the mind moving freely without the body, absorbing the solitude of rain. No one will try the road in here now or cross the river; no one can enter by television or telephone. Part of what gathers in pools is the contentment of being alone.

But it doesn't last long. In an hour the mist snagged on these ridges frees itself, and the sun flows back strong and yellow. The last of the rain trembles on the clothes line, flashing silver as it drops from sight. During the storm, the peach tree in the back yard stretched up thin and crooked, like a charcoal etching of itself. Now its leaves glisten like mica. A small brown spider is already repairing its web.

I heat a cup of tea and sit on the front porch. Barn swallows have abandoned the clay and straw nests caking the loft beams. Now they scissor through clear air, hunting for insects I can't see. The ground hog pauses at his burrow, observing my dog and me, then slides from his catacombs under the barn and into the weeds. Under the porch roof, wasps and bees continue working in undisturbed symmetry. Living in this house has been like holing up in a gigantic hive. The farmer and I took kerosene-soaked rags and burned out the yellow jacket nest in the chimney, and we knocked down a dozen or more wasp nests. Still, the insects will not give much ground. They have claimed this house for too long, and seem to know they'll outlast me here. But they are willing to coexist, these mud daubers, constructing homes shaped like little organ pipes. Carpenter bees as long as my thumb bore black holes into the porch wood. During the past month, they have become a kind of company. I don't know what I mean to them, but to me they are a discipline, a gauge of distance, an awareness of physical self.

This yard, this dirt, these trees are dynamic, continually shifting into fresh configurations. I hadn't realized before how little asphalt asks of you, how air conditioning atrophies the senses, how print can lock your eyes to a page. Here the world is rich and fluid, and fluidity is more exacting. I've begun to understand how difficult it is simply to keep track of my hands and feet. To forget a hand while opening the gate is to grab the red hornet sunning himself. How many years has it taken me to grow separate from this body, from the earth? I find I must move slowly and with concentration, or I'll get stung. Or I'll miss the lizard glazed with blue, who, crafty and scrambling, warms himself on the porch boards. How tiring it is to concentrate in this manner, how quickly the mind retreats to fantasy, to thought rather than observation. But I try, and for the first time in my life I can sit for hours and just look around.

Soon my dog yawns and stretches himself. The farmer is coming down the road. I've begun to appreciate why he moves so heavily, so responsibly, as if he's walking shoulder-deep through a pond. It has little to do with his almost seventy years, for field work has kept him supple and solid. But he watches the world and where he's going. He shouts a hello and hesitates by the gate, then reaches in his pocket and pulls out a letter. My mail has arrived via boat. Staying on this part of the farm has been like living on an island. The river carves an arc around three sides, while the forest erects a fortress along the back fences.

This is the world the farmer has chosen for himself. Some of his family have moved off the land, their children becoming teachers and doctors who return for a visit when they can. During World War II the farmer was stationed in England, and he's seen other parts of the United States, but he rarely wishes to travel. This farm is as much a part of him as his hands and his rituals. Over his muscled back he wears a shirt as plain as the dirt in his fields. Gum boots encase his legs, and a billed John Deere cap shades his eyes. Under it, his gray hair lies short-cropped and cool. He holds a walking stick and a burlap bag for carrying tools and vegetables. He has adapted to his land as much as it has been molded by him, and he is happy here. He can think of no reason for going other places.

With this wet summer, he often has long spells where he has time to talk. Walking up to the porch with a smile, he gives me the letter and asks if I would like to go with him as he checks his fields and cattle. I step inside the house and lace on my hiking boots, then grab the walking stick he made for me from a sourwood branch. We leave, securing the gate behind us. The dog bounds ahead, past the barn and the white oak shading it. We chat as we walk toward the river, and we pause at the head of the field. Where I see "pastoral-farms, green to the very door," he sees something else and says, "fescue, red clover, lespedeza, 1200 bales at harvest." At such times, I would like to walk a field plainly as he does. Straightforward, unencumbered. I need a guide here—a compass, a new language, a way to escape beyond the blinds of formal education. While the farmer has what seem to be his own limitations, at least they are different than mine. We both know that, and an unspoken respect has grown between us—and friendship.

He stoops to scrutinize the ground, marshy from the rain. It's the scarce fertile bottom land, where families have lived for generations, that would have been flooded by a dam proposed by the U.S. Army Corps of Engineers. This entire farm would now be under water. The project was one reason telephones have yet to be installed throughout the country. Until plans for the dam were cancelled in the 1970s, the phone company refused to service houses scheduled for condemnation and submersion. Phones now are promised for most of the lower Gorge.

While the Forest Service divides the Gorge into three main sections, local people tend to define it in halves. To them, the upper Gorge stretches from Sky Bridge to the river bridge close to Raven Rock. Considered more scenic by visitors, this section attracts the bulk of the tourists. Here, and on land further upriver, stream action and other kinds of weathering have eroded mighty figures through black shale, limestone, and resistant sandstones, forming the heaviest concentration of stone arches, rock houses, and other formations found east of the Rocky Mountains. The river twists around boulders big as cabins and cuts through valleys with cliffs several hundred feet high. It rushes past box canyons, sharp ridges, distant lookouts. A particularly rugged terrain distinguishes the area drained by Big Calaboose Creek, often referred to by old-timers as the Calaboose Country. It has long been called that, they say, because this territory is so wild and rough, the river so full of shifts and rocks that it all resembles a calaboose or jail—a place with no way out of it.

Because of the steepness and narrowness of the upper Gorge, there was never enough tillable bottom land to support more than a small number of permanent settlers, though the logging boom provided jobs for an influx of workers who mostly came and went with the industry. Today, only a hand-ful of people live there, and most of the land is owned by the federal government. As national forest, the area has reverted to wilderness, and few signs remain of homesteads other than the occasional clump of fruit trees—their bark curling and rotting, the names of their fruits forgotten, the hands that planted them long returned to the earth. Close by, you may find foundation stones quilted over with weeds.

The lower Gorge, however, is a different story. Spreading from the river bridge down to Bowen, this area does contain a few spectacular rock formations such as Courthouse Rock, Double Arch, and the Haystack; but the valley broadens here, unwrinkling itself into fields large enough to support substantial farms. Much of this land has remained privately owned, some staying within the same family since early settlement days. A sense of community continues among these people, and some semblance of tradition. Most of this would have been destroyed by the dam, which was stopped partially by ferocious grassroots opposition.

The early explorers of Kentucky, among them Dr. Thomas Walker, Daniel Boone, and John Finley, reached the mountains around the Gorge during the late 1700s. It was then that the legendary adventurer, John Swift, supposedly found and lost his silver mine in the area. After the Revolutionary War the first settlers also started arriving, some lured by land grants awarded for their military services, and they turned their hands and ingenuities to supporting themselves in a wilderness of forest and stone.

For instance, saltpeter was mined at numerous sites, particularly around the sandstone cliffs so characteristic of Red River. Here saltpeter or potassium nitrate could be found in a relatively pure form in dry caves and rock houses. Even today, if you look carefully, you might see drill holes or other evidence of these operations. As a main ingredient of gunpowder, niter proved especially lucrative to mine around the War of 1812, and to some extent during the Civil War, and this activity has left its mark in a place named Powdermill Branch in the lower Gorge.

The name Tarr Ridge indicates another early enterprise in the Gorge—the "running off" of pine tar. This substance was produced in kilns with 20 to 30 foot diameters, and used wood from the immense timber growing at this particular spot—which later was nicknamed "The Big Woods" by loggers. An important export item during the War of 1812, pine tar brought its highest price between 1810 and 1830; afterwards the market declined until about 1900, when it died out locally. People in the Gorge also used pine tar as a trade item for such necessaries as salt, as an ingredient in grease, as a treatment for livestock, and as part of a popular remedy for themselves—pine tar and honey.

Pine tar additionally proved handy to caulk the "coal boats"

built around Red River. While geologists believe that the thick
layers of coal found elsewhere in eastern Kentucky once
existed here, these were eroded away over millions of years by
the same process that carved out the Gorge itself. Though no
significant coal beds remained behind, spotty deposits close to
the surface were exploitable, if only by short-lived, single-man
operations. Some of the early settlers, who had such names as
Gray, Hon, Horne, McGowan, and Rose, were involved in
mining and boatmaking. One man, himself almost a hundred
years old, recalled to me how his grandfather hewed out boats
over sixteen feet in length, then transported his coal downstream, sometimes floating on the Kentucky and Ohio rivers
as far as Frankfort or even to Louisville in order to sell his
cargo. Afterwards, he faced a long walk home.

But it was iron, not coal, which played a more substantial
role in the Gorge. By the late eighteenth century, a furnace
was built on the "Great North Bend," and the Red River Iron
Works manufactured a variety of products, including cannon-
balls for the War of 1812. This industry required not only
considerable supplies of iron ore, but also charcoal to fuel its
fires, which created another demand on the nearby forest.
Over the years, a community sprang up around the Red River
Furnace, then located where Clay City stands today.

Aside from the occasional artifact or suggestive place name,
few traces remain of these settlers, particularly those who
stayed in the remote hollows upriver. They have faded away,
following the even fainter Indian cultures which preceded
them thousands of years in time. Those ancient native people
may have regarded the Gorge as a sacred place; and maybe it
would please them to see how little impact they had on the
sanctuary that sustained them, to know they have been erased
by wind and the subtle working of water. But who can say—
for while the imprints of their hands and the mounded scraps
of their existence may be discerned by the archaeologist's
explorations, their thoughts are irretrievable, save perhaps
through some dim communion of the imagination.

For many people in the Gorge today, living history extends
back two or three generations, or roughly a period of 100 to

150 years. This is the span of witnessing, of the primary exchange between incident and generation. To some—now old, but once children hearing the first-hand account of grandparents—time picks up after the Civil War. It was then that permanent settlers came to Red River in appreciable numbers, many of them attracted to the broader bottoms of the lower Gorge.

The ancestors of the majority of these people were British, as a short list of local names indicates: Ashley, Baker, Banks, Bowen, Brewer, Chambers, Childers, Crabtree, Day, Denniston, Duff, Farmer, Garrett, Gibbs, Hale, Halsey, Jones, Ledford, Martin, Mays, McKenzie, Morrison, Palmer, Peck, Quinlan, Sargent, Scott, Sexton, Sizemore, Skidmore, Smith, and Spencer. From what different families have told me, it seems that the ancestors of several of the larger landowners arrived in Virginia, where they remained for a generation before heading to Kentucky. Once in Kentucky, they lived for another generation elsewhere in the state, with several clustering in Harlan County, before coming to the Gorge. Some moved to acquire more land, others to avoid feuds springing from property disputes and from antagonisms sparked by the Civil War. Though Red River wasn't free from feuds, they were less common than in such areas as "Bloody Harlan."

I am thinking about these things when suddenly I realize the farmer is striding away. I follow him. His ancestors moved to the area not long after the Civil War, as did those of the next farmer who lives down the road a piece, on the more accessible side of the river. This other man, now in his eighties, has been a local leader against the dam. The last time I visited him, he trudged inside his house, hot from the fields, no shirt under his overalls, and sat tiredly in a rocker. After removing his hat, he wiped his wire-rim glasses and smiled. Then he began talking, a man used to speaking his mind.

"Most of the people who come early to Red River was from Virginia—stopped at Harlan County and come on. My grandfather, when my father was about twelve years old, come here in 1884, and they were farmers by occupation. But through other kin on my mother's side, I am one of eight generations of people who have been here for the last two hundred years, when Patrick Henry give land grants to this land. I have a copy here of some of the first claims on tracts of land."

He leaned forward and pulled several papers from stacks of newspaper and magazine articles, then drew his chair closer so I could see.

"I think you should look over some of these," he said, pointing to a xeroxed page. "There were 10,550 acres in the tract that my farm is part of. P. T. Roberts laid his claim in 1778 and Patrick Henry, governor of Virginia, gave him title in 1786. This was all part of Fayette County, Virginia at that time. Shortly after, Roberts and some Bowens—they must have been friends—come up here. Now there's Bowens all over this country, and the little town down here is named after them, of course. One of my mother's people married a Bowen, and that's how our genealogy goes back.

"Us people are not like lots of people. We've always been here, some one or other of the family, to keep the home fires a burning, and there's hardly ever one that'd sell a farm. If they do, chances are it'll be to some of the relations. We stay because of this great country—I don't think it can be matched anywhere. I know and enjoy so much of what is here that other people don't see. I want you to read something I wrote a few years back. I've got plenty of copies, so you can keep this one if you like."

With pride he handed me a paper. A few years ago he'd taught himself to type, so he could fight the dam in print, and many of the articles stacked around us he wrote himself. I read, while he sat, waiting.

Dedicated: To Save the *GORGE*, Our Heritage, Homes, Land And People, In The Land Of *EDEN* Of Our Ancestors

Dec. 25, 1975

MAN AND THE INSEPARABLE LAW'S OF NATURE

Yea though we reverend, Honor and adhere to Dec. 25th, as being the anniversary and birth of Our Lord Jesus

Christ, 1975. A.D. we are blessed 364 other day's of the year, in happiness, securiety, contentment, peace and joy, of the nesseties of life of NATURE, in the valley of EDEN, a primitive paradise in Red River Gorge. (Ky.) As I stand in awe this Xmas day, and view this priceless, primitive treasure of 60 million year's of *SUPER ARCHETECTURAL DESIGNING*, my soul is raptured with an endowment and inspiration to write that I have dwelled, eat, saw, and beheld, tasted and drank of it's many fascinations and fountains for 74 year's, I know feel and possess a pantheistic kinship to all *NATURE*, and as much a part of it, as the cliff's, flora and soil beneath my feet. If the ashes after cremation of my body were chemically analyzed? You may be amazed to discover the 14 major primary chemical elements identical the same that exist in this fertile valley.

WE SHALL NOT————allow this IRREPLACEABLE PRICELESS HERITAGE OF CREATION, with inspiring beauty beyond description, to pass from the face of GOD'S GREEN EARTH, by the folly of a hand full of people blinded in insanity of economics to build a Dam: This would be an unforgiveable SIN AGAINST GOD, NATURE AND ALL POSTERITY. *WE WILL*———— strive vehemically to see that it is preserved to be around at least the duration of another *ICE AGE*, and hopefully another governor————Hon. JULLIAN M. CARROLL, to guard and keep it that way.

I grinned, folded the letter and said, "You told them, didn't you."

He said, "Farming doesn't require too much education, but an education is good for anybody. It's like one newspaper said about me, 'He's only got a fourth grade education, but he knows what only a lifetime in eastern Kentucky can teach a person.'

"We beat the Army Corps of Engineers, and I believe it was the first time they was stopped after a project had already received congressional authorization. They wanted to drown us out for a recreational lake, take this farm away so people could parade around in boats. Or for what folks down in Clay City like to call flood control. Well, let me tell you something about that."

Though he was still sitting in his rocker, his voice rose and his cheeks flushed red as boiled cherries. "Back in '38 or '39 we had what was called the Frozen Flood and it was known about all over the United States. It was called that because it started up by Frozen Creek and the headwaters beyond Hazel-green and Campton. That cloudburst made the largest flood I ever saw, and thirty-eight people was drowned. Up there, the mountains is close together, with just a small valley. They said water come off the mountains ten foot deep—that's the reason so many people couldn't get away.

"Well, that flood come through here and went on down in the Kentucky River, and my family didn't lose anything. There wasn't nobody around here in any danger. All the people that ever built on the North Fork of Red River have always built out of the flood plain. Now, we grow crops on the flood plain, but we don't live down there. We're not like them Clay City people. They build on what belongs to the river. Naturally, they get flooded. That don't happen up here. But they want to keep their land and flood us out! We don't want no levees! We don't want no floodwalls! We don't want no channelization!"

He hesitated, then laughed. "Why, on this river here, you can grow anything that can be grown in the temperate zone in the United States. That comes from the composition of the different mineral elements of this soil, which comes down through the Gorge and all this area above here. We grow about fifty-some different commodities for home use. Course, when it's preserved and put up for winter, why it makes about 75 to 80 different eatable ingredients. So we don't have to buy much like some people do. This is our home, and we're staying."

As I left, he patted me on the shoulder and said, "Farming is all I ever wanted to do that's satisfying. You're making a living and trying to do it the best you can. Never compromise something that seems to be fair—I've always tried to do it better."

By now, the farmer and I have reached the other end of his hay field, where barbed wire slopes to the river and the dirt grits with sand. For a moment he rests a hand on a cedar post, and we both stare at the river. Its chocolate-colored water has swollen high up the bank from the morning rain. This is the North Fork of Red River, which runs through the center of the Gorge. The Middle and South Forks join with it farther downstream.

The farmer thumps the post and says, "You may not believe me, but once I laid a fence like this in the other pasture and took it over by the river. By the next year, that fence was buried—the river had put down new soil five feet deep. That's like putting money in a farmer's pocket, giving him free land! Backwater leaves the best fertilizer in the world, and I didn't mind so bad putting up another fence! Ever few years we get flooded and lose a crop, but it evens out. I'd say this river is our life line."

I believe him. I've often heard how families would clear hillsides so steep, the thin soil would erode away in a single growing season. And this is where it all ends up—here, and on down the river—this silt of farm, of the past.

Red River has been more than a "life line" for people. It and its tributaries also spawned great schools of fish, including white suckers, black suckers, hog suckers and bass, blue catfish, yellow cats, mud cats and channel cats, sunfish, red-eye, muskie, pike, perch, and the little flashing silverside. One old-timer recalled to me, "When I was a small lad, my father and I would go a seining. Some men had forty-foot, sixty-foot seines that would go in the river. They'd be a seining for muskies or pike, bass and red-eyes, and they turned the rest loose. There'd be so many suckers in that seine, they couldn't get it up on the bank. Even in places like Indian Creek, I saw maybe as many as 300 fish in one big hole of water. Today you can go up there and it's very doubtful you'll see a minnow longer than six inches or a foot. That's the difference between then and now."

Over-fishing, pollution, and such other short-sighted practices as gigging and grabbling have taken their toll. Gone are the days of the huge lurking catfish, when it took two men and a chain through the gills to hoist such a fish from the water.

Another good catch was the grayish white, soft-shelled turtle. According to some people, these were fried and served with biscuits and gravy, and tasted a lot like frog, or were made into turtle soup and sopped up with corn bread or crackers. Hard-shelled turtles tasted about the same, but were more difficult to dress. One man smacked his lips, remembering how much he had liked turtle eggs for breakfast.

Less appetizing were yellowish black eels. A man had to rub his hands in dry sand before he could keep hold of their slick sides. Then there were slimy, salamander creatures called waterdogs that could walk the banks and were considered a nuisance if hooked. For swimmers, black leeches might prove worrisome, especially where they collected around the submerged sides of rocks. These seemed particularly bad around Gladie Creek.

As well as supplying food, the river also provided transportation. Logging began in the Gorge during the second half of the nineteenth century and for many years the river was used to float logs to a sawmill complex downstream at Clay City. Crews of men would work in pairs, sharing crosscut saws. After a tree was felled and trimmed, it would be dragged or "snaked" by oxen, horses, or mules to the closest stream. Here, workers constructed splash dams by building pens on both sides of the tributary and filling in between with small tree trunks, branches, stones, and mud. Water backed up into a pool, which would be filled with logs. Usually the crew waited until after a soaking rain or when a "tide" or flood rose in the river. Then they knocked out a "key log" or "trigger," which released the water and carried the logs foward the river. Splash dams were located on Parch Corn, Calaboose, and Swiss (Swift Camp) creeks, among other places. An old logger told me that at one time splash dams held back every branch of Gladie Creek.

Elsewhere in Kentucky, workers threw together log rafts which they would ride to get their logs to market. But in the Gorge, logs were not rafted but "sailed" or floated loose. One man kept tools and other equipment in an accompanying boat, while others pushed stray logs from sloughs with spike poles and cant hooks. If the logs jammed, someone would shoot them loose with dynamite. The company that bought the logs would give a man credit for his work, then initial the log with a branding iron for identification. Depending on the current, it usually took a couple of days to sail the logs some twenty miles to Clay City. An early logging business of substantial size was the Kentucky Union Company, which later was followed by the Swan and Day, Broadhead and Garrett, and the Dana Lumber companies.

Sailing logs proved time consuming, inefficient, and too dependent on the weather. In the 1890s, narrow gauge or "dinky" railroads were laid to transport timber from such places as Chimney Top. Then, sometime between 1911 and 1914, the Nada Tunnel was constructed for the only standard gauge logging line built in the Gorge, and this development made possible further large-scale tree harvesting in the area, including the lower Gorge. During this period, another big sawmill operated near Nada. By 1925 the logging was finished, and the railroads began to be dismantled. The last was gone by 1942, with some of the rails being donated to the War Production Board as iron for artillery. Though the railroads and their loads of logs have long disappeared, their presence survives in such place names as Railroad Hollow, Switchback Hollow, Bandmill Bottoms, Boardtree Hollow, and the Big Woods (Tarr Ridge).

What was it like to grow up in the Gorge, especially the upper Gorge, during the boom years between 1880 and 1925? A woman born at the turn of the century tried to describe it to me: "Honey, I was born over at Chimney Top and there was eleven of us children. My father was a foreman on the railroad, and he helped them haul logs out of all the Gorge—Gladie, Chimney Top, Wolfpen, that whole country. Me and him used to have wonderful lovely times together. He nicknamed me Buck. 'Buck,' he'd say, 'You want to go a fishing or a hunting tonight?' We didn't have much to entertain us, only we were just a joy to one another.

"When I was a little girl, we would get moss and make the prettiest great big pillows and beds. There's a kind of tough mud, and we'd make mud cakes and trim them with red shumake berries and the prettiest blue briar berries.

"On Sunday afternoons we would hunt mussel shells. Years ago we used to have a lot of mussels in this river, and I've wondered since whatever become of them. We'd pull the poor things apart and have the awfullest piles of them! Some would be pretty and pink inside.

"Then we moved to Rush Branch, and it wasn't a thing in the world but just a wide place with a little log house set in the mouth of it! But we had a good place to raise plenty of corn, beans, potatoes—a garden and our molassy patch. Nowadays they hardly ever raise that—cane in a cane patch to makes molasses or what some calls sorghum. They grind that juice on a mill, and a horse will take it around and around. Then they got an evaporator, or a pan they call it, a setting on a furnace. That'll boil this juice down until a man knows when it is a turning into molasses. Then he'll go to skimming it—many a one of us stepped in the skim hole! They got a great big hole dug out, and he'll skim some of that old green foam, some just as green as poison. Then when it gets a little bit done, it turns yellow, and when it's almost ready to pour out through a strainer into a can, it'll be almost creamy white. Many a time we'd all be a prancing around, getting in that molasses pan, cutting us a paddle and eating the foam, and one of us would fall in the slop hole and have to go to the river and wash that nasty old foam off our legs! You know, if you don't just exactly pay attention—but a bunch of kids will forget about the hole and down they'll go!

"I did what was called feeding the mill. I'd just pick up them stalks two or three at a time, poke them in the mill, and the old horse just going around and around, the yellow jackets a swarming and the wasps—anything that'll smell that sweet cane juice—and if I haven't got stung to death!

"We raised a big cane patch every year while we lived on Rush Branch, and of course we had our chickens, cows and hogs. We had a good living, but we didn't have the goodies in life we've got now.

"Then we lived over on Wolfpen in the Gorge about three different times. The railroad went clear to the head of that main holler and they logged it out. There was a big boarding house the company had to feed all their men that worked in them woods and on the train. We lived up the creek, and then just below the mouth of it for a while.

"Then the company took the steel out of the tracks and left those crossties in, and great crowds of young people would gather and sometimes we'd walk clear to the heads of them hollers. Them days the government didn't have much to do with anything, and we'd just cut big birch trees and scrape the sap, and it was the finest stuff to eat that ever was. We'd go a fishing, some would swim, go for long walks on Sunday, a wading in the water. A lot of us would go a boat riding wherever we took a fancy on those long streams of water. Then we'd meet at a house where they had a victrola with a great big horn, and, oh children, we thought that was the grandest thing that ever was in this world. Sometimes the house would be crowded. And songs—they're such crazy old things. Ever now and then I hear a snatch or two they used to play, but I can't hardly remember the names of them. Anyway, honey, we wouldn't listen at them now.

"So, Wolfpen was a beautiful place for a while. People kept it all nice and clean, no underbrush, no weeds. See, when the railroad went through there, why then it was a wide spaces of bottom, and people lived ever two steps nearly in little old houses because they's lots of works—cutting timber and working those big log trains that come in there. Two trains ever evening would take out four or five carloads, and that was a lot of help to the young men. They would cut logs, or roads to the logs, where they'd hollow them out with cattle or mules one. They had them great Perchen [Percheron] or Norman horses with feet bigger than the bottom of that stove almost.

"And families lived from the head of Wolfpen to its mouth. Lord, I just can't hardly remember the amounts of families

that did live there, it's been so long since the works went out.
My daughter was born in 1921, and the works had done went
out then, and it was long, long years before the timber got big
enough to cut again. I'd say it took about four years to cut all
the timber from up Wolfpen, Chimley Top, Gladie, and then
clear on through what's called Laurel Branch, a country we
used to live in too. Where all the works used to be is wilderness
now, and you just hardly couldn't believe it. But when the
works went out of there, honey, they all had to leave, move out
after the works and go one place and another."

The farmer has studied at the river all he needs to and has
turned away. This spot is not far from where he sets his
overnight lines for catfish. If he's lucky, he might hook a few.
As we walk, he quizzes me on the names of the trees we're
passing—his way of teaching, having fun, and showing me
where we're going. I'm amazed how he can identify trees
solely by the color and texture of their bark. It reminds me of
lumbermen, who in the old days, could just look at a stand of
timber, one perhaps covering several acres, and accurately
estimate the number of board feet contained in the lot. These
feats range beyond my ken and seem to require an additional
set of senses, and I can't help wondering how much of the
natural world has become vestigial to us in the last hundred
years.

So we name sycamores and haws, pawpaws and locusts,
hemlocks and buckeyes, sassafras and sarvis, and those trees
valued by loggers—white oak, black oak, yellow poplar, pine,
lind, ash, and birch. Then come the trees sought both for their
wood and nuts—hickory, hazelnut, walnut, and the beech
with its little three-cornered nuts so prized for fattening hogs.

We've been skirting the pasture where the forest begins,
but the farmer will not enter it, and he uses his walking stick
to poke into high grass before stepping down where he can't
see. His stick is not an affectation, for the farmer, like most
people I've talked with this summer, has a real and seemingly
constant fear of snakes. Guide books to the area downplay the
presence of snakes, but local people think differently. They try

to avoid any place that looks "snakey," which means virtually everywhere during this season, particularly in August when some believe snakes leave the ridgetops for the cooler creeks and river—closer to where people live. Children are kept playing by the house where grass is short. And they are nagged to be careful. All the times I've camped in the Gorge over the past years I never saw a snake, yet in the last ten days, I've almost stepped on two copperheads.

It's as if in this garden, this vast puzzle of trees and ridges and vines, that the snake remains the last natural enemy. The forest itself was conquered fifty years ago, though with the help of the Forest Service, it has sprung back with a vengeance. The large animals of the forest, however, haven't returned, though they still linger in the folk-memory and in such place names as Bear Wallow Ridge and Wildcat Creek. One man had this to say: "Along about the time I was born, the big animals disappeared from this area. That's when the last wolf was shot. It was killing pigs, and everybody was after it. There's a creek up there called Wolfpen, and someone built a pen there to catch this wolf, I think now. Anyway, I always assumed Wolfpen was named that way. I really don't know if they caught the wolf in the pen or not—all this was handed down from generation to generation. That's how we know about a lot of these things.

"But there was a fellah that lived in Gladie, sometime around the Civil War or later. They had those muzzle-loading rifles then, and he already had his loaded. He saw this old wolf in the valley below his house, and he took aim and got it. And that was the last wolf killed in this country."

According to other sources, during the late 1800s a group of wealthy farmers from the Bluegrass bought approximately 2,000 acres in the Gorge for hunting and fishing trips. This included land around Fishtrap, Dunkan Branch, Gladie Creek, and Copperas Creek. One man over eighty years old recalled for me that his grandfather had caught bait and acted as a kind of guide for these people.

In those days mountain lions also roamed the hills. One of these animals was described to me in almost supernatural terms as a huge black creature that may have killed a man or at least fed on his body. Another man, born in 1921, recalled that "this country was much wilder then—no roads, no cars, and very few people lived there. We continually had fear of snakes, but also animals would be killers, especially if you cornered them. At that time there were still a few bear and a few panthers. These panthers were grayish brown and had big green eyes something like a bobcat. They were like a leopard in the face, and they were long, slender, very smart, and very, very fast. They were killers, all right, if they got on a helpless child."

"In the early 1930s the government built this highway through there. The WPA mainly built the roads. When they made this one, they also set up ranger stations and a lot of forest men moved in to patrol the whole country, protect the animals and all that stuff. It was then the animals moved further back in the mountainous areas. Some probably moved completely out of the state. And of course, the hunters and trappers had killed a lot of them by then."

At one time bears were plentiful, but I had to talk with a man almost a hundred years old to find my first witness. He remembered a bear hunter who had killed dozens of them. He said, "I never did see any live bears up there, but I seen the last bear killed on Red River. An old man found one in a hole at Eddard's [Edward] Branch, run it out with a pair of dogs and killed it with an old hog rifle. I never did see the hide, but I seen the man a peddling the meat. People bought it to say they'd eat bear. I never did eat any of it—I didn't have fifty cents! He was getting fifty cents a pound! I was about sixteen years old, so it's been done over eighty years ago. That was the last bear killed in Kentucky, I reckon."

A man forty years younger recalled other details about this bear hunter. "Back in the 1920s I can remember hearing the old bear hunter. He killed two big bears, and one weighed close to 800 pounds. It attacked him at a cliff ledge. I guess the old man was telling the truth, the way he told the same story for years. He was hunting at the head of Chimley Top and going around a cliff with nowhere else to go, and I guess this bear had young ones up there and come at him. He killed it with an old muzzle-loader rifle, and I think they got a mule or sled to haul it all the way to Nada. Different people told me they seen it at that time—probably back in the early 1900s. It had to be a big bear to weigh that. He had their skins."

Claiming to have found their tracks, a few people insist that bears still inhabit the remote reaches of the Gorge, though no one I've talked with has seen the creatures themselves. In what people say and how they say it, however, they seem to have a need to mythologize these animals, to conjure them up and somehow reconfront them, for they were a measure and a challenge, a perception and a skill, and they are gone.

But the snake remains—slithering, deadly, everywhere in their eyes. Any poisonous snake the farmer sees he'll destroy out of principle, though its existence adds an edge of excitement to such a walk as he and I are taking. As might be expected, the snake has been a center for folklore in the Gorge:

a snake injured during the day will not die until night;

if a green garter snake bites you, you'll die of laughter;

rattlers and black snakes can "charm" birds and small animals;

two types of rattlers infest the Gorge, the more deadly one being almost black in color;

black snakes will kill rattlers and other poisonous snakes, so they are handy to have around the yard and barn;

cow snakes suck milk from cows;

nonpoisonous snakes leave a straight trail; poisonous snakes leave a crooked one;

snakes move at night, when it's cool and they are not easily seen;

if a snake bites a pregnant woman, it can mark the baby;

a snake rattle put inside a fiddle will help its tone.

One story told to me emphasizes the belief in the snake's supernatural power. As I heard this account, I realized I'd read a similar tale in books on Appalachian folklore, and this underscored for me the pervasiveness of these superstitions: "You know, Grandaddy had a story about a snake that I've never been able to forget. This one was about a little girl who went to the rock pile to eat her milk and bread every day. And he said she begin to lose weight and get pale and was sickly. The mother followed her down to the rock pile one day, and the black snake came out. She'd take a bite of bread and milk and then give the snake a bite. Now there's a cow snake that's suppose to suck milk out of cows, but we know snakes don't eat vegetation. Anyway, the child kept looking more sickly all the time. Whether she was getting poison from the snake or it had hypnotised her, I don't know. I just remember that was one of his stories, and all we had was his word about them."

In a few remote churches in the area, snake handling has been the ultimate demonstration of faith and of expressing the spirit of God. Though it's now illegal, people admit that on rare occasion this ritual is still surreptitiously practiced. One day I sat talking with a woman known for her kindness, humor, and good cooking. This great-great-grandmother's face was smooth, round and tan as a gourd; and her hands never slowed from peeling apples so small and wormy that most people would have thrown them away as worthless. She had much to say about faith, religion, and serpents.

"Back years ago in the Gorge they would have what we'd call cottage meetings. They would go from house to house like they did in olden times, breaking bread like the Bible tells us—that's breaking the Bible, the word of life. And an awful lot of good was done. Once they had a big association at a log yard back in there. They called it a log dump then, and it had thousands and thousands of logs they'd hauled and decked there. Then when a big tide would come in the rivers, they'd dump all them logs and float them to wherever they had a sawmill. So once they had a big association at this log yard. People come from far and near and they'd have a preaching service. They'd have singing, music and dancing! And then they'd have what's called dinner on the ground. Course it was on tables and things, but that's what they called it—meeting all day and dinner on the ground. And people got saved.

"If I were to give you my testimony, it'd scare you to death. I could tell you things that'd almost knock your feet out from under you! God took me out of the very jaws of death. In fact, I was a going out into eternity, and really, if I'd of went out at that time, I'd been lost. I wasn't saved. But oh, the goodness of the Lord! How many trials, how many tests, how many bitter heartbreaking things I have went through, but God has seen me through victoriously. Yes, I like to always claim and praise Him as my wonderful savior. And I'm telling you one thing sure—when you're facing death, and you know you're lost if you was to go out, and God brings you from the darkness into His marvelous light, it really makes you believe. Boys, I praise Him today above everything on earth.

"I had an inward goiter on my neck that a doctor in Stanton treated me ten years for, and I had got to the place where he'd be giving me such strong medicine my hair felt just like straw. He would feel my hair and diminish the medicine so many drops, from fifteen to three, and finally I had to quit all together. Then I went to a revival one night that'd just started up at Slade, and when they anointed me with the oil the Bible speaks about, and the saints laid their hands on me and prayed, it felt just exactly like a bolt of electricity. It hit me right in the top of the head and went through my throat, down my arms, down my body and right out to the ends of my toes. And boys, you talk about somebody that was instantly healed!

"Now the greatest thrill on earth is watching somebody handle serpents. It really makes you believe, because them snakes is so deadly. I've only seen them use copperheads once. Usually it's rattlers, so you've got to be filled with the Spirit.

"One weekend, boys went back in the woods and caught rattlers they was sure hadn't been handled before. They got six big ones in a box. Now a woman had been anointed in the church in the morning—anointed means that the Spirit has come down and filled you. She run all over the church and handled snakes. Now that evening she acted like she was anointed again, but she wasn't. A Brother warned her—this Brother-preacher felt fear. The spirit of the Lord made the danger known to him and he warned her. He said, 'If you're anointed, you have no more fear of picking up those snakes than you would of taking a cold drink.' But she didn't listen.

She put her hands in the box and immediately was bitten. She died around midnight. Over her heart come a big thick purple bun or pancake where the poison gathered—it was purple like a tame ground cherry. And as she died, she told us to keep up the practice and not let down on the doctrine because of her. She had disobeyed the moving of the spirit of the Lord.

"There's still some snake handling around here, but not much. The community and the law stopped it. And people wouldn't wait for the anointing of the Lord. But when they do, watching them handle snakes is the most wonderful experience in life."

Folk remedies for snake bite seem to abound almost as plentifully as the snakes themselves. Bottles of turpentine are kept handy, from the belief that turpentine held over the bite will draw out the poison. In the past, ooze made from red oak bark was thought to have the same effect. Another treatment was to make a paste of soda powder and water. This would be smeared on the bite until it turned green with venom. A poultice brewed from boiled peach leaves thickened with corn meal also was supposed to lessen the poison and swelling. Other concoctions with water weed (*Impatiens capenses*, also called jewelweed and wild touch-me-not) were thought to be helpful against poison ivy as well as snake bite. Crushed water weed or crushed burdock soaked in milk were used as remedies for dogs struck by snakes.

The farmer and I have finished circling this pasture. The ridge above us is crowned by an intricate arch formation I've wanted to see for weeks, but the farmer will have nothing to do with attempting such a climb. We would have to bushwack for half an hour through briars, rhododendron, and other heavy undergrowth, and who knows how many snakes might be waiting along the way. Besides, the farmer's shirt is creased and freckled with sweat. The morning is getting steamy, and he has yet to check his cattle. He must notice the stubborn way I poke my stick in the dirt, for he cautions me against walking alone. He may not return to this side of the river for two or three days. If I get bitten, there will be no one to help. I'm still not convinced, when I realize that I, too, have been warned by a kind of brother.

Back at the house, we rest for a moment at the well, pouring long cold pulls of water, sweet and deep from the earth. But the farmer doesn't tarry. He's had his say. Wiping his face with his hat, he takes up his stick, and heads down the road to the next field.

August 3, 1979

During the day, the ridges circle this farm like the rim of a huge cup. With these and the river as boundaries, the fields seem cut off from the world—a place of squirrel and hawk, of deer tracing patterns just beyond the trees, a place worth exploring if only from the cane-bottom chair on the front porch. But as night approaches, these hills block the sunset. The trees seem to rise with them, poised against the sky, ready to crash with nightfall. At the very last light, the tin roofs of barn and silo and corn crib hang luminous as foxfire, floating in the darkness. Then, they too disappear. From the woods, an occasional whippoorwill cries or an owl screeches.

I go to bed with the sun. And a long-barrelled, Smith & Wesson, .38 caliber revolver. Its hollow-nosed bullets could tear away part of a door and knock down any intruder, even if I'd only hit an arm or leg. With such a weapon, I probably could have blasted out the Nada Tunnel in a week, rather than the months it took two crews to complete the job. I sleep with this monstrosity loaded and pillowed not six inches from my head. No wonder I'm never quite sure if I'll wake up from these nights, or just hear thunder rumbling in some distant dream. Despite such a fear, I couldn't have stayed here and slept without a gun. This way I sleep, but I sleep rigidly.

For someone who has never lived by herself, this place has been quite a challenge. The nearest phone is a half-hour drive away on this side of the river, and now I don't even have my car. I keep it parked across at the farmer's next to the gravelled road, so travelling through the Gorge is a much shorter trip. But the farmer has only one boat, and I must wait for a ride. My closest neighbor, he lives almost half a mile away and on the other bank. In case of any problems, especially at night, I'm on my own.

During the past weeks I've found that the Gorge, like the

rest of the world, has many fine people and a few trouble-
makers; and, like elsewhere, few places here are actually
inaccessible. The old road back to this farm has a reputation
for being rough in more ways than one. Because it is little
travelled, it proves attractive for drug parties and drinking
sprees. Three weekends ago, a man was shot near Face to the
Wall, and last Sunday morning I walked down the road only to
find the gate and that end of the property snarled and twisted
shut with barbed wire. I couldn't have driven out if I'd wanted
to. Was this just a practical joke meant for no one in particular, or was it a warning directed at me? There is no way to
know.

Not long ago at a grocery in Slade, a man leaned close to
me, confidentially purred my name, and hurried away. I had
never seen him before. The people I visit these days seem
worried that I stay alone here. Each of them in turn warns me
to be prepared for trouble, and I understand their concern and
friendly advice. An unfamiliar woman living by herself, especially in such an isolated spot, attracts attention and talk,
and not all of it can be good. I keep thinking, however, that I
have double protection as a guest on the farm of one of the
oldest, most respected families in the area. To bother me
would be to cross them. This seems as strong a preventative as
any law or weapon.

Tonight I was asleep when the dog jumped and began
barking. He sounds a loud alarm, but by nature is no fighter,
and sometimes he seems nervous because I am. Tonight,
though, I hear a car slowly grinding by the house. It doesn't
stop. Now all I can do is wait—the rain has continued this
summer and the river is deep, the ford uncrossable. Any car
which passes must return, sooner or later. My clock glows
11:30. So I lie in the dark, stuffy heat, aware of the stillness of
wasp wings, the pant of the dog, the sudden eerie creak of the
gate, my misinterpretation of wind, the complexity of shadow.

This side of the river has had a bad name for years. In the
past, families lived down the road who were clannish, whose
activities were secretive but not secretive enough, and who
were avoided because of their brutality. A woman friend
described one of them to me:

"A family lived up there that had four sons. And the father, Titus, nearly beat them boys to death. We'd be on top of those ridges picking huckleberries and hear him whipping them with a horse whip—just sounded like rifle shots. His wife was a midwife and a good woman, and I remember how much we liked her. She lived with that man until he finally took up with a younger woman and moved into a shack on up the river somewhere. There was no end of people a moving into them little hollers, you know—kept building little shacks and log houses, moonshining and making rot-gut. So that's what he was doing. I don't know where his wife and those boys ever went to, but they left and I never heard of them no more.

"And finally this younger woman left him. He was making bad moonshine with some character he'd taken in. Ever body was always afraid of Titus and wouldn't have anything to do with him if they could help it. He had a reputation for all kinds of things. He once killed a rattlesnake and swallowed its heart. It was supposed to make him brave. He said it came up three times, but the last time it stayed down.

"Anyway, he and this man got to drinking and fighting one another, and Titus beat him unconscious, rammed a shotgun up his rectum, shot him, and left him for dead. The man wasn't found for quite a while, then somebody hunting found him—the odor drew them. So they figured out what happened, but Titus had left this country. I never heard of him anymore, and of course nobody wanted to hear of him. But that pitiful family he raised—they were kind like their mother, humble, and of course deathly afraid of him. There were a few families like that scattered around in the hollers off away from other people, families ever body avoided."

The river then formed a social boundary. Before the 1930s, people highest on the social scale lived closest to the river where they could make a legitimate living, farming the bottom lands or sharecropping on someone else's property. The farther back in the hollows a family stayed, generally the less they were known or trusted. Any living on ridge tops tended to be highly suspect.

One of the oldest attorneys in the area told me that he

thought the roughest times in the Gorge were between 1900 and 1930, when one or two murders a year were brought to trial in Stanton, the county seat of Powell County, which includes part of Red River. During that period, only a sheriff and two deputies had charge of law enforcement, and they had little choice but to let folks back in Gorge "work out their own problems." So justice was often a privately handled affair. Despite sporadic "thrill killings," however, he knew of only one lynching, which occurred at the beginning of the century, and only one legal hanging, when a husband was convicted of murdering his wife. One man killed another in Bowen and received only a five-year prison sentence. After he was released he murdered his second victim, and was sentenced to seven years. But usually such hard-boiled characters disappeared from the area, realizing that either the law or the community would be after them.

What most frequently attracted law officials to the Gorge was not murder, but moonshine. While early settlers brought a knowledge and tradition of distilling with them from Britain, practicing it for their own enjoyment and benefit, this activity didn't gain full momentum until Prohibition in the 1920s and early 1930s, when a large national market paid what seemed like enormous prices for anything resembling whiskey.

The Gorge proved an ideal spot to moonshine. The area was riddled with small, isolated hollows. Most had a spring or branch running through them, which provided the fresh water necessary for distilling. The few paths that served as roads into the Gorge also worked to the moonshiner's advantage. Such inaccessibility further concealed his movements, and made detection and apprehension by authorities more difficult. If corn—gritted, parched, fried or baked—was the staple of his diet, it was corn in the form of liquor which put cash in his pocket. An abundance of this crop could be grown in the fertile bottoms of Red River, but getting it to market at Mt. Sterling or Winchester was laborious. Corn liquor was easier to transport, and the return on the dollar was much higher.

Money also could be made by informing, and during the

1920s citizens could be paid up to fifty dollars for reporting the location of a still. Such tips, however, often were made anonymously by letter—both by disapproving neighbors and by those hoping to lessen competition. After receiving such information, the sheriff might make an arrest by himself, or might take a federal agent with him. Seldom would a federal agent venture into the area by himself.

One man in the Gorge explained the situation this way: "The revenue men and the law cracked down on the moonshiners worse than they did murderers in the early Thirties. See, when the government legalized their own liquor, that was one of the few revenues they collected taxes on. So things between the moonshiners and the revenuers could get pretty tough. It's like the story I heard on a record way back in the early Twenties or before. A revenue man showed up at a mountain home where he knew a moonshiner lived, and told a little girl playing in the yard, 'I'll give you five dollars if you'll tell me where your dad and his still is. As soon as I come back, I'll pay you.' The little girl said, 'No sir! You give me my five dollars now, cause when you go up there, you ain't coming back!'"

The old-time attorney recalled that if a moonshiner was going to be caught, often he was better off arrested by a federal agent. He then could be tried in federal court where, if it was his first offense and he was otherwise a respected person, his sentence could be probated. On the other hand, there was no probation for any offense in state courts in Kentucky before 1934. Here a first offense for moonshining, in 1922 for example, brought a minimum fine of $100 and sixty days in the local jail, or could cost as much as $500 and six months. If a prisoner couldn't pay his fine, he had to serve it out in jail, working at hard labor at one dollar a day. A second offense was considered a felony and could cost a man one to five years in the state penitentiary. The unlucky third offender faced a two- to ten-year sentence.

The attorney estimated that a dozen or more moonshine cases were tried per year in Stanton during the 1920s, but that no more than a fourth of the people who moonshined at any given time were caught. Most of the moonshine was produced here on the North Fork of Red River in the Gorge. It sold for one dollar to $1.50 a pint or eight dollars per gallon. By the time it was transported to Winchester, the price increased to ten dollars. Most of this liquor was produced for the outside market, with people coming from Louisville, Lexington, and Cincinnati to buy it.

One man recollected quite clearly to me what moonshining in the Gorge was like at the time. He said, "There were moonshiners by the hundreds in this country. We made it, and practically ever body else did, because it was the only way you could actually get any money—at that time and in that area. But ever body had a tight lip as far as squealing on their neighbor.

"In those days, a lot of moonshiners were killers. Some pretty bad eggs would make rot-gut and put battery lye in it, anything to make it stronger and cost them less. And they were poisoning people. They didn't care if they killed you or not, just as long as they survived and made their little money. Also, there were quite a lot of killings done by moonshiners and bootleggers among themselves, so people were afraid to report them to the law. So the revenue men were continually looking for stills, cutting them up and destroying them.

"Another reason people were afraid to squeal on each other for moonshining is because they were doing it too! Either you dealt in it or you made it—that was the main source of getting a hold of a little cash. Otherwise, ever thing was traded from one thing to another. Very seldom did you ever see any cash, except by dealing in whiskey.

"So, as I say, in those days a good percentage of mountain people, one way or another, dealt in whiskey. A lot of those who made good stuff and financially set themselves up, bought big farms and homes, and cars which were rare at that time. Most of the people who dealt in liquor was the only ones who could afford a car. The ones that wound up broke or in trouble were those so-called rot-gut moonshiners who made bad stuff and had no market finally for their goods. They'd go out of business, and the ones who took pride in their trade and made the best liquor usually prospered financially. A lot of those you see living in fine brick houses today, their money was made and paid for back in the Twenties or Thirties by parents or grandparents who dealt in whiskey.

"When I was a boy, ever chance I got I sipped, getting into my dad's or brother's whiskey. All kids seem to want to try anything strange, so to drink it was strange to me. To see it made was not strange. I got drunk my first time when I was only eight year old. I was at my brother's still, watching him make liquor. He left me to watch the fire and as soon as he got out of sight, I took a cup and got into the backings. That's when it's half whiskey and half beer—before it's run off in its final state. Anyway, I drank three or four cups and got so drunk I passed out. My brother carried me home and when our parents wanted to know what happened, he told them I had took a chew of tobacco and got sick!"

Another old-timer leaned back on his porch one day and laughed as he answered my questions about moonshining. "Sure, the boys would usually have some moonshine around! But I never did know of a woman or girl either who drank it when we was growing up. Why, I didn't even drink coffee until I was twenty-two year old—I drunk moonshine! There used to be enough moonshiners back here to keep you in all you wanted to drink! It got so good, I couldn't hardly stop till I got drunk! If somebody got rough with the whiskey business and someone knew where a still was, they'd report them and the law would cut their still up. Back in the Panic Days during the 1930s, corn was only getting thirty cents a bushel, but you could get a whole lot more if it was made into moonshine! That was about ten dollars a gallon! And you could carry it easier to market—if you didn't drink too much of it! Of course you couldn't sell it on the market, but to a bootlegger, because it was illegal.

"At that time, all legal liquor was called government liquor, because it was taxed. It was also called red liquor because they colored it. Good moonshine, if it was made right, was clear. I guess that's why people called it white lightning. And that green liquor—if people didn't know or care what they was doing and used a bad rig—if that moonshine had a greenish cast, then you'd better not drink it! Why, I can remember during Prohibition days when they were running around with hair tonic or something they called jake-leg—they'd have to shake that leg in front of them before they could put it down.

"Now if you got hold of some sugar-jack, you might drink it of a night, go to sleep, and wake up in the morning with nothing but a headache. But if you got some good corn liquor, why you could wake up and feel foxy for two or three days. It'd just keep going real fine! Good moonshine was the best drinking that there ever was. I even remember buying a quart for a dollar. A quart! Course, that was forty or fifty year ago."

Moonshining was mostly a male occupation, and only rarely would women moonshine or bootleg. Many strongly disapproved of it, but realized it was a practical necessity. As one woman admitted, "Momma hated it that time Dad made whiskey. She came around tight-lipped, trying to keep it hid from the children, but she had to let him do it." Other women appreciated certain side benefits from the art of distilling. One laughingly confided, "When I first married and was living in the Gorge, I didn't know nothing about cooking. But then, of course, I started getting interested in that and also in working on the farm. In them days my husband didn't have no work hardly, and now I'll tell you what he done. It's a very bad thing to say, but truth is truth. He used to moonshine a lot! They would get rid of it as quick as they made it. Well, he used to have so much sugar that he'd bring in, you know. He did run off a lot of corn whiskey, but he also made sugar whiskey out of sugar and meal. He'd always give me all my sugar out of the two or three hundred pounds he'd get at a time. And I'm a telling you! That's the reason I started canning—making jellies, jams, preserves, and all kinds of pickles. I just had bushels of sugar. Then we started buying jars, and sometimes I'd have way over a hundred quarts canned."

Perhaps because of its illicit and clandestine nature, its excitement and daring, moonshining in the Gorge generated a number of humorous tales. From the late 1800s up to the 1920s, blind tigers dotted the area. These make-shift shacks served as pick-up points for buying moonshine. Their name originated from speakeasies, which during Prohibition Days were often referred to as *blind tigers* or *blind pigs*. In the Gorge, blind tigers sat by roadsides and were kept closed except for a small opening about countertop high. Money and liquor were exchanged through this, so the seller's face remained hidden. That protected him in case he was indicted in front of the grand jury. If the shack was located on someone else's property, the dealer usually shared a percentage of his profits with the land owner for his unacknowledged cooperation. One old-timer remembered seeing the logging trains which passed not far from his house. A blind tiger also stood close to the tracks. On Fridays, the engines would stop, the men would pile off and crowd around the blind tiger, make their purchases, then merrily jump back on the train, all set for the weekend.

Some moonshiners in the Gorge were more reckless than others. One stuck a sign outside his place which read, "Moonshine for Sale." According to a local person, he was never arrested, because no revenuer would take the sign seriously. Another moonshiner took his product to Morgan and Wolfe counties to sell. A big man who rode a small black mule, he would tie a couple of kegs behind the saddle, then wear a huge raincoat to cover them. When he'd leave, only the mule's head and tail could be seen sticking out from under it. When he returned, the coat was folded and put away.

One day I was talking with a man about moonshining and he had a good story. He grinned and pointed to some joe-pye weed, a long-stemmed purple flower that grows wild and thick in the fields. Breaking a stalk and handing it to me, he said, "Around here, this plant's called queen o' meadow—see how it's hollow all the way through? It's about the only plant I know of that ain't solid at least at the joints where the leaves is. Well, my pappy told me that when there used to be a lot of moonshining going on in this country, people'd hide their kegs till they needed them. Now if a man was out in his fields and got thirsty, or he knew where someone else hid his liquor and he wanted to sample some on the side, then he'd cut one of these queen o' meadows and suck out as much as he wanted through the bung hole. It sure comes in handy to know such things!"

Superstitious tales also gathered around moonshining. One account told to me by a man in his late seventies included the ghost of a big silver dog. He said, "A young man and his uncle were moonshining over on Haddon Ridge about forty years ago. One night they were making a run to South Fork, carrying their liquor and riding two mules. As they stopped at a gate, the young man saw a big white thing approach in the moonlight, eight to ten feet long and that looked like a huge silver dog. It ran under his mule's belly, but the mule didn't even sidestep. The young man shouted to his uncle, but all his uncle did was turn in the saddle and say, 'Boy, you just scare too easy. Pay no attention to such things and you'll not see them.' The young man could still see the silver thing moving up the mountainside, but he began to doubt his eyes. Later, though, he talked with other folks and found they'd seen the same thing."

One of the most interesting folktales I've heard in the Gorge was related to me by a woman in her sixties. It concerned two brothers who were moonshining and is a good example of the ghost stories one often hears in the Appalachian mountains: "There was a big land owner on Red River that had two sons, Billy and Frank, and four daughters. His wife died young and left him with the children to raise. Well, he couldn't seem to do much with those boys. Instead of helping on the large farm, they begin moonshining, drinking a lot, and fighting with one another over money when they'd sell their moonshine. Finally, Frank killed Billy, shot him to death at that moonshine still. And Frank immediately began to drink himself to death, just drunk all the time with remorse and the loss of his brother. The way it all happened preyed on his mind, and he was drinking himself to death.

"He was working some place where he had to come home at night. Maybe he was still moonshining—I really don't know what he was doing. But he had to pass the family graveyard before he got home. It was close to the road and about a half mile or more away from the house. As the story goes, when he'd ride past this graveyard, the ghost of Billy would get on behind him, ride the horse, and hold onto Frank with cold hands until he got to the stiles that went over the front yard fence. Frank would get off to hitch his horse and Billy would disappear.

"And Frank kept drinking harder than ever. It was worrying him to death, and he was frightened and scared to within an inch of his life. He wouldn't speak or try to communicate with Billy, but he knew what it was because it would happen as he passed the graveyard. He would feel him get on the horse and come up close against him cold. So he began crying over it, would cry all the way home—of course, he would always be drunk.

"One night before he got to the stiles, he thought he'd try to ask Billy not to bother him, that it was driving him crazy and causing him to drink himself to death. So he said, 'Billy, I know that's you. And I know what I done to you. I'm sorry that I killed you and wish I had you back.' And he said, 'I'll do anything if you'll not bother me any more.' Billy held on and there was no answer, of course. But when they got to the stiles, Billy disappeared and it never happened again.

"Now that's all I know about that story, but I've heard it many, many times. When I was a little girl was when it happened, I think. I knew Frank well, but never did get to know Billy, so I must have been very little when it happened. Frank wasn't too old a man when I was eleven or twelve—I guess he was in his early thirties. They had a great big white house and I remember how pretty it was when we first moved to the river. They had all kind of out-buildings, and the hillsides were beautiful and green and well cared for. But the place begin to go to wrack and ruin. By the time I was big enough to notice—well, fourteen or fifteen—the house begin to turn gray and the porch to sag, the stiles begin to rot down. Nobody seemed to know much about them. They were kind of a clannish family, and not many people socialized with them."

After the end of Prohibition, moonshining began decreasing in the Gorge, though one source told me stills were being seized and destroyed as recently as the 1960s. Though Powell County was wet until 1938, today Red River is dry to its bedrock. A few bootleggers stay in business, but little sign remains of the moonshiner and his ancient trade, except in the place names of Revenuer's Rock and Moonshiner's Arch. If a person wants to buy alcohol legally, he must drive to Mt. Sterling or as far away as Lexington. In many homes around the Gorge, liquor is not kept or discussed, and for religious reasons is considered a great evil. But on a night like tonight, great quantities of it must be consumed by someone, given the piles of bottles left strewn on the ground.

It's these spirits and their effects on people which frighten me more at a time like this than the supernatural kind. But lying here, waiting in the darkness, I think about the superstitions and legends I've heard this summer. How much easier that is to do than to think about the faceless car creeping up the road, of time seeming to pass as slowly as mold creeping up the wall. Ghosts are easier to confront, as folks in the Gorge have been doing for years. While a Dark Hollow near Dunkan Branch can be found on official maps of the area, I've heard talk of a Bugger Hollow not far from Cloudsplitter, and of other crooked, narrow places that seem "hainted" but whose locations are as difficult to pin down as the spirits themselves. A woman friend described one of these spots to me:

"My uncle was a fine-sensed man, and I believe he told the truth about this. He said one night as he was coming home from somewhere on his horse, he saw a little old woman in the Greasy Branch Holler. She was dressed in white, but she was headless. She appeared out in front of him, just a dazzle in the air, and all at once disappeared. Now he told us that, and I don't believe he would have dabbled around in telling such a story because it wouldn't have profited him to do it. Anyway, from then on everybody called it the Dark Holler, the Bugger Holler, or the Haint Holler. It's been about sixty years ago, and that's the first I ever did hear it called that, and I've always heard it named that ever since."

A man took me aside one day and told me about another

hollow with "a thing that run people away from it." He said, "Down in this Bugger Holler, where the hill went down by the river and there was a dip in the road, there was a noise of people, but nobody could never see them. And a lot of folks heard that. Really, me and my wife heard it ourselves. We was walking through there in the day time, and all of a sudden it went like a big congregation of people just a coming and talking. We sat down to wait for them to pass and see who it was, and apparently they got right at us, but then they just vanished. We took off down the road looking for them, but there was no tracks or nothing."

Another tale also told as a true story contains the traditional folk motif of being buried alive. A woman recalled the following incident that occurred while she was living in the upper Gorge about fifty years ago. "Something happened once that we never have accounted for or been able to find out the answer to. My people weren't very superstitious. They were sensible. But one night me and Momma and Sis was working on a quilt. I believe we had it up on a frame and was sewing on it. I was about ten years old at the time, and my daddy and three brothers went coon hunting. Let's see, about a quarter of a mile up the creek from our house was an old, two-room shack that nobody had lived in for a long, long time.

"It was a dark night, misting rain like today is, only pitch black. We looked out and saw my daddy and the boys come running, carrying the lantern. We could see the light. They were running hard as they could, and they burst upon the porch and into the house and said, 'What's wrong! What's wrong! Who's hurt?' And we said, 'Why, nothing's wrong.' He said, 'There was a woman screaming. I thought someone was killing you.'

"They were pale as ghosts, just as white as they could be. Scared to death. But as they begin to talk, they remembered that a man lived over in that shack once who was mean to his wife and beat on her a lot. Finally, nobody ever saw the woman anymore. People begin to get curious and asked him about it, and he said, 'Why, she died with the flu and I buried her out there in that cedar thicket.' There was a cedar thicket close to the shack. Then that man run away, disappeared. Nobody ever knew where he went to. And they dug her up. She had turned over in her casket and had torn hair out of her head—her hands were full of it.

"My parents begin to remember that old story about him having beat his wife unconscious and buried her alive. As far as we know, if that wasn't the ghost of that woman scream-ing. . . . My daddy had hunted those hills all his life and knew the sound of wildcats and hoot owls and screech owls, and he said it was nothing like that. It was a woman screaming, screaming just horribly, and there was nobody that lived within two mile of us. Momma would ask him, 'Did it sound like it was coming from this house?' And he'd say, 'No, it sounded like it was coming from the cedar thicket, just a little bit above our house.'"

Other places in the Gorge were not haunted, but had legends attached to them. The best known tale is that of John Swift, an adventurer who in the 1760s supposedly discovered a great silver mine in the Gorge. As the story goes, Swift lost his eyesight during the American Revolution. Despite his written directions and journal entries, neither he nor anyone else could relocate his treasure. This account, however, has attracted miners, fortune seekers, and lone "surveyors" to the Gorge for decades. A few local people still think there might be some truth to the matter. As one man told me, "I'd say a friend of ours has found that mine. They dug down to where they come to a place where it had been a furnace in time. Said it had cinders and was about ten to twelve foot wide and twenty-some feet long. He had lumps of silver as big as your finger and said it was ninety per cent pure silver." None of these rumors has panned out, however, and the only sure sign of Swift left in the Gorge is found in such place names as Swift Camp Creek and Silvermine Arch.

The Gorge has its own lover's leap at the Jewell Rock. According to local legend, a man by that name jumped to his death there after being spurned by his sweetheart. Pinch-Em Tight Cliff, another high point in the area, also has inspired some tales. Because of its height and narrowness, some say it was a favorite haunt of moonshiners, who could see approaching revenue men in time to escape.

One grandmother offered this explanation of how Pinch-Em Tight got its name: "Years ago, I guess even years before my daddy was born, there was an old woman and her family that lived way up one of those hollers in Red River. Some called her 'Devil,' 'Devil Sal,' or 'Devil Woman of Red River,' and she was supposed to have been very mean to her family. She made rot-gut moonshine and beat her children pretty badly. I've always heard she killed her husband, and nobody who lived in those hollers would have anything to do with them.

"They had to get on top of Pinch-Em Tight Cliff. There's a crack that goes up just a very steep slant, and in the middle of this crack is a very narrow place, and in another place there's a great big boulder. We picked huckleberries on top of that cliff many times and gathered pine knots to burn. I remember how Momma used to scramble over this big boulder first and drag us little ones after her. At the tight place we didn't have any trouble getting through.

"Devil Sal took her whole family and went huckleberry picking on top of Pinch-Em Tight Cliff and had two great big ten quart buckets. So they had an awful time getting her through this tight place going up. Then they got her buckets full of huckleberries and started back down. She made the mistake of letting all her children go first. She came last, and as I said, she was very mean to them and I doubt they had very much feeling for her. Anyway, coming down she got in a twist some way in this narrow spot. She had slipped her buckets of huckleberries up on her shoulder so she could brace herself and she got in a twist in there. She couldn't get loose and the family ran off and left her. And she stayed in there several days until she lost enough weight, I reckon, to get down through the tight place. So they called it Pinch-Em Tight ever since!"

A few old-timers in the Gorge still believe that unborn babies can be "marked" if the mother is frightened during pregnancy. One woman blamed her fear of swimming on the fact that it had been bred into her. She explained, "A lot of people don't believe in marking anybody, but before I was born, my mother let my older sister fall in the river. My mother grabbed her by the dress tail as she was going down her last time. And I've always had a horror of water because of this."

Many years ago, another woman was bitten by a black snake while she was picking wild ground cherries. She was deathly afraid this would mark her unborn child's face with black splotches like the snake. Luckily, it didn't happen. Another family in the Gorge, however, was not so fortunate in a similar situation. A friend gave me her version of the story: "This man had two sons, twins, that were badly retarded. They crawled on all fours and growled like bears—they couldn't talk, you know. He would explain to people that before the twins were born, his wife was sitting in the house, sewing. And he slipped up on her, dragging a bear he'd killed with him, and threw it across her lap. Scared her and marked the boys. I've heard people tell about going there. I never did go. People said that the family'd cook everything in the world, twenty-five or thirty different dishes if you would go and eat with them. But they would let those boys eat out of bowls with their hands, and nobody could stomach to eat there."

Other superstitions involve animals and insects. Some folks believe if hornets build their nests close to the ground, this indicates an "open winter" with little snow, or that no bad flooding will occur in the upcoming year. Mourning doves are sometimes referred to as "rain crows" from the belief that their call is a sign of rain. As it turns out, this superstition is at least a century old and widespread, relating to a variety of birds in many parts of the world, including Scotland, northern England, and the American Ozarks.

One woman carried the idea of prophecy a bit further. She recalled how her father was walking in their yard when he saw a large yellow and black spider spinning a strange-looking web. He stepped closer and watched. When the spider finished, it had spelled WAR. A few months later World War I was declared, and the family was convinced the spider had tried to warn them.

Suddenly my dog is barking his own warning. In a few seconds I hear the car returning. Now it stops. I lay my hand over the gun and wait for the slam of car doors. I wait some more. In a couple of minutes the car revs its engine and bumps away. I listen to it go. The dog circles back on the floor, the clock glows 2:45, and time begins piling around me again in single black leaves.

In the morning when I get up, I find that I left the outside light burning all night, and moths as variously colored as shells seem stranded on the porch. A luna moth looks paralyzed, its wings as green and delicate as seaweed, while another gleams like mother-of-pearl. A few lie under the light, shriveled and brown as dried kelp. By a porch support, I see a long winged roach, black and shiny as a waiting hearse.

Across the river, the hills have receded, washed back by the fog. It's safe to turn off the light.

August 20, 1979

The road past the house seems even narrower this morning. I slide the gate shut behind me and turn in the fog toward Euliah Branch. This is the beginning of my goodbye to summer, to the Gorge and to my friends here. Before I leave, though, I want to pay my respects to a few people I haven't met.

As I walk, things drift by in the fog—Queen Anne's lace, blue chicory, dried blackberries on their briars. Kettle spiders have spread their tentlike webs on the grass. In a bank by the road, a locust tree exposes its roots, and a hornet's nest dangles among them. Below it, in tractor tracks half-filled with water, tadpoles squirm as I pass them—no inch of this land is not ingenious with use.

I hear the crows before I see them, their calls grating in their throats. They sail past, dark and unflappable, and I envy them. Their eyes can penetrate the fog so much farther than mine, it's almost as if they don't need to see to know where they're going. The cattle must be grazing nearby. Their mouths whoosh and their teeth click in the grass, and the smell of fresh manure soaks through the mist before their slow redness does. And smell of wood rot, dank leaves—I cross Euliah Branch on its pure rush to the river.

To the left of the road, a field slopes toward Red River. Here the farmer has begun gathering his hands of tobacco, stabbing each one on a tobacco spear. But the patch is empty this morning—it's too early for him to be working yet. Fence posts emerge on a rise to the right. They're what I've been looking for, and I duck through the wire sagging between them.

A tombstone leans against the fence, whiter and more solid than the fog. It looks like a replacement stone for a grave nobody could find. It reads, "Rebecca Johnson, 1865–1945." Around 1865, saltpeter was mined not far from here for use in the Civil War. But she wouldn't remember that, and anyway, who can guess where she was born. All I know is that someone thought she was buried on this hill at the age of eighty, three years before I was born. I stop for a moment, thinking about her and other mountain women. What do I know of them, those who worked and died in these hollows, the hands of some growing harsh against their children, the heads of some bowing toward rest which never came until they reached here, the bodies of some weathered as these fence posts, the lives of some emptying and enduring beyond those of the men struggling beside them? I remember the women I've talked with in the last months, some older than this century—a few ancient ones, bedridden, lying in a loneliness that must be greater than death, but who nevertheless can tell of lives they do not yet regret. One or two still shine, even in such solitude, pure and trembling and somehow beyond their one hundred years. How little I can see of what they see. They pass ahead of understanding.

This graveyard is mostly weeds, poke big as saplings, their red stalks rising seven feet in the air, their wine-colored poisonous berries clustered around them. And ironweed stands almost as tall, purple-topped and keen-leaved. I push aside a clump of high grass. Nestled there is a small marker with a lamb on top, an innocent stone. Clay Mason, dead in 1899 before he reached two years old. In script below the lamb is written, "Sweetly Sleeping."

Nearby, another stone has a marble dove with a broken wing. The child belonging to this grave lived long enough to wear a vest and have his picture embedded in his gravestone.

It shows a boy with serious eyes. He has "Gone Home," the stone says. How many children died so young of the "summer complaint" or other ailments that moved faster than a doctor could travel or had the skills to cure? What did a woman feel, laboring to bring such a soul into this world and knowing all her pain would likely be for nothing? How often did a man guess as he hammered together a cradle for his son that within the year he would be piecing together his coffin, that this life would be encompassed by the wood in his hands? Surely he could look around himself and notice how four or five children out of a dozen usually did not survive. How did such deaths shape a person's sense of the future, or was the future even given a name by those who lived in these hollows?

And where are the fathers in this graveyard? In the far corner a thicket of weeds is taller than I am, and I turn to my right. I've forgotten my stick, and I'm afraid of snakes. I don't want to join these people. The cedars overhead—their branches hang scraggly as old men's beards, and poison ivy mats their trunks, hairy vines twisting up from the ground. Finally, I see a stone, squarely masculine. I know it says "Father" before I can read it: "Charles Whitlock, 1896–1918." The letters cut harshly into the granite. 1918—that year a flu epidemic killed more people than the world war. The Gorge proved no safe pocket from either. When he died at the age of twenty-four, what burdens did Charles Whitlock leave behind? What wife, what children stood disbelieving in front of this stone, or were they secretly glad? What house rotted down and fell back into the woods from which it came? What path disappeared in weeds as this grave now disappears? Who remembers the hands of this father? Did they sweat over corn or cover the face with emotion? Did they slap at people or slap in time to music, or both? What kind of a man was he? Who could know that, even while he lived. The acres of this farm once supported a dozen such families and cabins. So little sign is left, so much seems without origin.

Past this grave, most of the stones are toppled, a few almost completely buried with only their tips protruding. One lies heavy and round, like the discarded anchor of a ship. Here and there, the ground frets choppy and rough where a grave has sunk. The last stone faces west, thin and worn and speckled with moss. The only inscription is a carved hand, the index finger pointing skyward. I follow its directions and look up. The river fog is rising. When it's gone, the day will be scorching.

I slip back under the wire, pant legs wet to the knees, boots drenched with dew. The fog is breaking into gold coils against the sky. Bell flies and snake doctors already fly bright and fast in the air. I climb down the bank toward the road, clay sticking to my boot cleats, and walk back toward Euliah Branch, lost in thought.

At the house I brew some tea and sit on the porch. What good is this meditation, I ask myself, staring across the yard. The martin house high on its pole was empty when I arrived in June. It's still empty. The churn-dashers, their little flowers white as milk and shaped like the cross-sticks of a churn, still bloom in the grass. Rock doves still peck at stray grain by the corn crib, their cheeks marked with black exclamation points. Suddenly they fly into the trees.

A green sedan rattles up the road, the first car to come through here in a week. A fat man is driving, his wife and two children waving and smiling so friendly as they pass. Most likely they'll be back. It hasn't rained for several days and the river may be fordable. But I doubt it. The noise of their engine fades so quickly, I could have imagined them. Soon I'll be following them, with some of my most important questions unanswered. Why did I feel I knew this place when I first arrived? What ties me here now? Why does most truth worth knowing always seem just beyond reach?

"Because of the way you think and see," a man says. He's sitting on the porch swing across from me, his face pale, his eyes displeased. I know this man. In July he showed me a secluded part of the upper Gorge. He hadn't visited there himself for years, and without warning he disappeared for half an hour, gliding away under the trees, a shadow. Then he reappeared, moving the way I imagine Shawnees or Adenas scouted through here. Silently. I tried to follow his trail but couldn't. Then he stopped and showed me where ginseng and yellowroot grew, and how to sap birches and carry their sweet strings in wahoo leaves. He uncovered powdery huckleberries and the shiny pellets of bearberries. He told me how to set a lure for coons and mink and then how to kill them. He waited for my talk, but I had little to say. That satisfied him, and we left for the car.

"Who cares about what you know or don't know," he says. "That's the way it is."

He watches me, his thin body rocking in the swing. Glancing around, he says, "Take this house, for instance. You know Green Garrett was born in that middle room, and he felled the great trees in these parts. The next family that lived here had no children, but they gathered young people around them and square danced all night. Their lives were long over before yours started." He looks back at me expectantly, almost in kindness. I just feel sad. So he nods, points down the road toward Face to the Wall, and says quietly, "In two days you'll leave here and not come back. But you'll remember what I'm telling you, and you'll do with it what you want.

"In the 1920s when I was a young man, much younger than you are now, Route 15 come through this country. It was named the Trail of the Lonesome Pine and it's still called that today. It started at Winchester, passed not far from here, went through the coal fields and deep through the mountains all the way to the Virginia line. When I first remember seeing that highway, it was just dirt road, not much different than this one. No gravel, no surface, no nothing. It was graded off, but just plain dirt. Car wheels would grind the dust so fine and so deep, it'd be inches and inches of solid dust. Therefore, the whole mountain and all the trees and everything on either side was white with dust. Instead of green, it would be white, that whole mountain—just white. Look, can't you see it?"

I feel that dust in my eyes, rub them, and he's gone.

PART TWO

A VIEW FROM CHIMNEY TOP

I never tell a story the same way twice,
but I tell the truth.
LILY MAY LEDFORD

This woman doesn't fit this room, this comfortable house in Lexington, Kentucky. Her sitting here seems unexpected, as much about her might be—her six-foot height and deep, almost manly voice, the hickory eyes in a face both sensitive and determined, and not much changed by sixty years. After finishing her coffee, Lily May Ledford clips her fingernails to play old-time banjo, music which has taken her from sharecropping in the Gorge to playing on Broadway, from picking on home-made instruments in Pinch-Em Tight Hollow to performing before the king and queen of England at the White House.

She blunts one hand and begins on the next. "I should have known you'd want me to play too," she laughs. "But Lord, you know how slow I am in the morning." As usual she is appreciative of attention, something she hasn't always had. Born to Daw White Ledford and his wife Stella May Tackett in 1917, Lily May was lucky just to survive infancy. Four of the fourteen children didn't. Yet, despite a harsh life on Red River, by the time she reached her early twenties Lily May was lead performer for the Coon Creek Girls, a group generally regarded as the first all-girl string band on radio, appearing with such stars as Red Foley, Woody Guthrie, Burl Ives, Pete Seeger, and Orson Welles.

The living room reflects little of these experiences. A color television blocks the fireplace, and the velvet couch and stuffed gold chairs complement the carpet and drapes. "You know," she says, leaning back in her black-and-white flowered robe and lighting a cigarette, "many times I have sat here, and the Coon Creek Girls and everything that happened—none of it ever was. It was just a dream, or not me at all. Then someone like you comes to see me and hear me play and I know that it did happen, is still happening, and my music does matter. Just sometimes it seems so long ago, and I guess a lot of it was." She stares off for a second, smokes, then adds, "Maybe we should find those photos and papers before I drag that banjo out, don't you think?"

She stubs her cigarette and heads for the bedroom where she opens a drawer. "I can't keep track of all this stuff. I need a

scrap book," she says as she heaps clippings and manila
envelopes on the bed. In the living room she deposits the heap
on the coffee table and settles in her chair, a picture in hand.

"That's Momma and some of us. Papa may have taken it.
For a time he was what was called a Sunday photographer. On
weekends he'd go around taking pictures." She stares at the
square so dark and worn with age, the two lines between her
brows deepening, though she is about to chuckle.

"As I've told you before, I was born on South Fork of Red
River, and when we first moved to the Gorge we lived at Gladie
Creek for two or three years. Then we moved to Chimney Top
and stayed for about five, but it seemed like a whole lifetime.
There's where I call home more than any other place.

"My daddy, he loved his uncle Joe Ledford who owned a
great part of Red River in the Red River Gorge, including this
Chimney Top area, this Pinch-Em Tight where we lived. We
were sharecroppers, and our house there had three rooms
which were fairly large. In the front room where Momma and
Daddy slept was a bed for the littlest ones—the fireplace kept
it warmer in there. In the other room the four boys were
fighting and sleeping in one bed. Us girls would sleep with
more little ones at the foot of our bed, and boy, that's the
warmest sleeping in the world—get into a corn shuck with five
people! And on bad cold nights, our cousin Pearl, who also
lived with us, would put every quilt she had on us. Most were
made of overalls and old coats.

"We had a lot of fun out of those corn shuck beds. The boys
and Daddy'd bring in sacks of corn shucks, and sometimes
we'd use a fork to tear them. But Momma said they'd pack
down too hard when we got them too fine, so she liked us to
tear them with our fingers and leave them an inch or two
wide. They made the best beds. In the summertime, we
carried them out nearly ever day to air in the sun, and we
renewed them every year.

"Momma had two bed wetters in me and my younger
brother, Coyen. We wet the bed until we was great big, and
she tried ever thing in this world to stop us. She wouldn't let
us drink water before we went to sleep, or she'd boil egg shells

and have us drink the water from that. Course, I had kidney trouble and I'm sure mine had something to do with it. Maybe it was psychological, too. I don't know. But she thought boiling egg shells and drinking the water would stop us, and it worked fairly well. She also made Coyen and me sleep together for a while, which we hated worse than anything because we were pretty big, eleven and twelve years old. He'd sleep at the foot and I'd sleep at the head, and we'd kick one another. If we'd wet the bed, each one would blame it on the other. But she'd make us carry the shuck tick out every morning and sun it all day, because we just couldn't have a new bed fixed ever night. And finally the day come when we just stopped.

"This house at Chimney Top was down in the valley close to the creek, nearly a mile's walk from the river. We lived at the foot of Pinch-Em Tight mountain and holler, and a branch ran by where we got our wash water. At the foot of the steep part of the mountain was a stream where we got our cooking water, and then up the hill where the source came from, was a cold-spring, just as cold as ice. It came out from under the hill, and Daddy dug a big hole and carried gravel to keep the water purified. Momma would make us carry the milk up that steep mountain twice a day in the summer, and bring back the ten-quart bucket of drinking water. There was always plenty of water.

"Two times we had lemonade. Daddy went to a railroad tie-making camp way out on a ridge to earn some money. There was sawmills throughout the country, where the logs would be hauled. My daddy was supposed to be the best tie-maker they had. He was much in demand and would make them just as square as they could be with a broad axe, and as smooth as if they'd been planed. He'd stay a week and then go to the store that wasn't too far, and always bring home a few little goodies we hadn't had to eat—maybe some cheese and a loaf of bread, and a poke of candy for us little ones.

"So he would get lemons so we could have lemonade from the cold-spring. Aw, it was great. And he would buy sugar when he got some work like that, but it'd be by the hundred pound. It'd come in fifty pound sacks, I believe, and the boys would take the sled as far as they could get it. But it wasn't every year we could get hold of much sugar.

"So there was fourteen children by and by. Poor old Momma had a child every year, you know. If it hadn't been such a rich, rich country it would have been impossible for us to have lived on what we raised and give our Uncle Joe his half. But the woods was full of nuts and the woods was full of berries and all kinds of things to eat and beautiful things to look at. There was mushrooms you could eat—we called them morels or 'dry land fish.' My daddy was a great hunter, fisher, and trapper so we were able to get at least nearly enough meat to do us. For fur he trapped foxes, mink, muskrat, possums, skunk, and weasel. Wild cats really didn't bring much—it was kind of sport to catch them, they was such fighters. We lost one of our best hounds to a bobcat—it cut his throat and cut out his eyes at the base of Chimney Top Rock. Daddy carried him all the way home, but he died shortly after that. Things like trapping for a lot of people, including us, was our only survival in the winter, so he trapped anything he could catch.

"The soil was so rich and so black and so deep that the vegetables we raised were great huge things, and the Lord was with us. He provided. There was times when we didn't have much to eat. Maybe we'd eat all our good canned things and our pork from the hogs we slaughtered by January. From then on it was dried pumpkin and maybe shucked and dried beans. We raised our own cane about every year, so we'd have sorghum and maybe some kraut and pickled corn. Even that would run out along about the last of March. Then we'd live on wild greens and fish until we got our gardens coming in.

"There was a school three miles away and across the river there at Chimney Top. My daddy made his own boats and boats for all the river people. He was very talented in wood craft and was a fine carpenter. He would set us across the river in his boat every morning and we'd walk the three miles. Then we'd come and holler—sometimes he would be off checking his traps and would be a little late getting to us, and I remember how cold it would get and how mad we could get at Papa!

"So it went on that way for five or six years at Chimney Top—that's my home. And I would fight like a tiger—if they ever started building anymore dams there or even think about it, I'll go to any measures to keep that from happening, because it's one of the prettiest places in the world. Now, it was a very, very hard life, but such a happy one. There was no television at night. There was nothing to do but tell stories, all the old stories my daddy and mother would tell. We'd roast potatoes and chestnuts in the fireplace and we'd pop corn—we raised our own popcorn—and make popcorn balls by sticking them together with sorghum molasses, and my daddy played music. And it kept us so close together."

While Lily May talks, her fingers sift the air to mark important phrases and her eyes light up, warm as pine knots burning. "Did I ever tell you about Grandfather William Ledford? He was such a story teller that some people didn't know whether he made up some of the tales he told or not. The way I remember it, he left home when he was fourteen and wasn't heard of again for twenty years. He'd rambled in the West during gold digging times, I guess. He caught a covered wagon train as far as Mississippi and worked until he owned fifty acres of river land. Long afterwards he came back and told us he'd married a woman there and 'she was barren and bore me no children and therefore'—that was the old-fashioned way he talked—'therefore, I left her and gave her all that I owned.' Then he caught another wagon train west to California and this time he said he lived with an Indian family in a hollow redwood tree, and they were Democrats. He became a Democrat himself, and Papa thought that was where he heard the name Daw White which he would give to my Daddy. Then he came back and married my grandmother, and there wasn't nothing barren about her! He played the fiddle left-handed and said he could pick the banjo right-handed. He was a very old man when I was six.

"The Ledfords probably settled in North Carolina when they come from the old country. A few of the younger Ledfords have said we come from Holland and the name was originally Ledderer, but some of the old Ledfords, Grandaddy and Uncle

Joe, said we were Scotch-Irish. Then we have a strain of
Cherokee that shows up in Coyen, I believe, and in my sister
Minnie. My mother's people, the Tacketts, settled in Virginia
when they came over. That family went into mines and
railroad work all the way, and they finally settled in Pike
County, where she was raised until my daddy married her.

"Some of the Ledfords went to Tennessee, and some settled
in Harlan, Kentucky, where my daddy lived as a boy. The
family must have come over awful early to work their way
finally to the Red River. My great-grandaddy owned nearly the
whole river, from the tunnel through the whole upper Gorge.
That's what I've been told. Thousands of acres—and he gave
each of his boys a farm. There was Uncle Ballanger and Uncle
Henry, who grew to be rich, and Uncle Joe who bought them
all out. Then there was Grandaddy, but he just didn't care. He
was like my daddy, you know. He let fate take care of things.
And he fiddled.

"So finally, Uncle Joe ended up owning all the land. By the
time I got into radio around 1935 or 1936, he'd sold a lot to the
government for $1.25 an acre, I believe. But he kept Chimney
Top where he'd built a home to live out his life. It was a
two-story house, had water piped into it, and they drilled for
oil. This would have been in the late 1920s. There were oily
places all through that country in swampy places, especially at
the foot of the mountain where Chimney Top Rock stands.
Uncle Joe hired an oil rig to come in, and of course they
believed they would strike it. My sister Rosie stayed with them
at the time and helped Aunt Bell wait on the drillers—she
boarded them while they drilled. Rosie helped cook, wash,
kept the beds clean—that was what they called a 'hired-girl'
job, and they paid her two dollars a week which was the going
price. So, they drilled for a few weeks and finally struck
gas—where there's gas, there's no oil. Their disappointment
was deep and keen, but at least they piped the gas into the
house to cook and heat with, and they used it for their lights
for many years. On South Fork where my daddy worked in the
oil fields, they've been pumping oil for over sixty years and it's
still going. Anyway, what a time Uncle Joe had building that

house. They had a piano and heavy oak furniture, and a lot had to be sledded from the top of the mountain, or carried by hand, on horses, in boats—I don't know what all!"

If her father didn't have the money of other Ledfords, he offered his children a wealth of musical ability. For Lily May, the ballads and mountain shout songs of her childhood were more than a hobby or casual entertainment. They gave a musical center to her family and made life bearable, even social, in the Gorge. Her father also shared his imagination with them. It didn't put food on the table, but it sustained.

Lily May glances at the picture a final time, and sits back to smoke again. Shaking her head at the half-filled ash tray next to her, she nevertheless pulls out another cigarette. Then she opens a drawer stuffed with picks, old banjo strings, scraps of paper with messages, and more matches.

"Times weren't always so hard for my family," she continues. "Once it was different. Before we moved to Chimney Top, Daddy had worked in the oil fields in western Powell County and he run two power houses, a kind of white collar job for that work. Sometimes he'd wear a tie and white shirt and jacket. And he always wore riding pants and leggings, and a billed cap. So he was a sprucy-looking man, and handsome. He earned good money for several years, even before I was born. This was before we moved to Uncle Joe's land when I was still very little.

"And he took a notion to throw a big Christmas. Now Christmas was usually sadder for our parents than it was for us little ones. But this time! He had ordered himself a false face with a white cotton band around it. He'd dressed himself in a long slicker black rain coat, and even bought new gum boots so they'd be pretty and shiny. And he wore black gloves. He went to the barn to do all that, unbeknownst to us children.

"He dressed his sled and horse about a mile away from home and waited till after dark so none of us could catch him. Our old black horse named Belle had a white star on her forehead, and he blacked that out with soot so we wouldn't recognize her. He'd bought red crepe paper to decorate the sled and disguised it with holly and cedar, and put everything in the world on the horse. Our grandpa lived just a hop and jump from us, and Momma went over there to sew and wouldn't let me or Sis go with her. They'd made him a great big bag with a strap around in front.

"We had our Christmas tree set in the middle of the floor over by the fireplace, with the chairs and all pushed back. He'd bought candles and Momma had tied them on the tree. We'd always string popcorn and make paper chains, but this year he'd also bought a few of them glass balls and some tinsel, something we never had again. So the tree was great big and pretty all the way around. And Momma had told us Santy Claus was coming that night. He wouldn't jump down the chimney, but would come in his sleigh.

"Soon we could hear him. He had different sizes of sheep and cow bells just a tinkling and a ringing. Then Momma said we could go to the window and look out.

"It was snowing as it had been all day. Ever thing worked just right for Papa. And as we looked, the horse and sled drove up all decorated and the bells stopped. The two older boys were just giggling—I know now they knew exactly what was taking place, but they acted like they didn't. Then out jumped old Santy Claus. He reached back into the sled and grabbed a bag that had great big things sticking from it. They were nickel sticks of candy—red and white striped peppermint over a foot long and wrapped. He came up the path, stomping snow and a whistling. Then he knocked on the door, 'Hellooo!'" Lily May's voice slides into the heavy bass of a man shouting. "'Helloo!'

"Momma made us sit and said to the oldest, 'Kelly, go open the door for Santy Claus! And us children was just quaking, me and Sis especially. Rosie and me was hunched up in the corner. And he came in with a 'hello and a ho-ho.' He did that so well. He was an actor, we found out then, with his other talents. He made the best Santy Claus that ever was with his laughing and 'a what's your name young man?' He shook hands with Momma first, then with the older boys, and then with us little girls. And I remember me and Sis were afraid to take hold of him, and he said, 'Aw well, little girls are bashful.'

"Then he said, 'First we're going to have a little song.' He sung a verse, and I remember two lines." Lily May laughs, leans forward and sings:

> Tree on the trunk, trunk on the tree,
> Prettiest little lights I ever did see . . . .

"He'd hit two more lines, and he'd dance and slap his hands all around the Christmas tree. Then he'd come in front again, sing another verse, and dance three or four times around and around that tree.

"Then he said, 'I guess it's time to get out the presents. All you children, from the oldest to the youngest, line up.' He showed us just how to set and he gave out to the oldest boys first. And they were giggling and snickering—Kelly, Joe, and Custer, all three.

"And he said, 'Have you been a good boy this year?'

"'Yes, sir.'

"'And did you bring in wood, and drag poles down from the woods and saw them for your mammy when she asked you to?'

"'Yes, sir.'

"'Did you saddle the horse when she wanted to go someplace, and did you do your feeding? And did you help in the corn crop and the garden?'

"'Yes, sir.'

"And he drug it out until he got down to Sis and me.

"'Now what's your name, little girl?'

"'Lily May.' He asked ever body their names as he went.

"'Have you been a good girl? Did you pick up chips and kindling and bring it in for your mammy when she asked you to?'

"'Yes, sir.'

"'Have you sassed your mammy and pappy this year?'

"'No, sir.'

"On and on he'd go. And as he questioned each one he'd say, 'Now, come up and get your present.' For the boys he had a pocket knife, a sack of marbles, a package of firecrackers and a packet of caps for the cap pistol. Each one got the same, I remember. Then he got to us girls and he said, 'Now come and get your present.' Sis went up and got a big doll. Boy, I like to lost my breath. It had on a red dress and white apron and some lace that I'd already seen at the house. They'd buy dolls undressed in those days—half-cloth and half-bisque. Both of us got a doll just exactly alike.

"Then he said, 'One more little song.' He sung a verse, danced around the Christmas tree and danced out the door, a-wishing Merry Christmas to ever body, jumped in the sled and took off, the bells just a-ringing.

"He left a present for Momma, and she opened it after he was gone. It was a long lavender silk dress, trimmed in lace and covered with pinkish cherries and vines for the print. Prettiest thing I ever saw. And Momma said, 'That's so beautiful, I'll never have anywhere to wear it.'

"The next day we baked chicken and stacked apple cake and pies. Had two or three kinds of potatoes, and a little of ever thing she had canned and dried went on the Christmas table. But the big hen or rooster she baked for dressing was the main thing we didn't have ever day. That was just once a year. Then the boys got out and enjoyed their cap pistols and firecrackers all day. Daddy took them rabbit tracking and hunting in the afternoon, teaching them how to use a rifle. Then Christmas was over. It only lasted Christmas Eve and Christmas Day. The tree was taken down—we blew out the candles just as soon as Santy Claus was gone, you know, for fear of fire.

"I'll never forget that Christmas and how poor it got after we moved to Uncle Joe's on Red River. Papa still worked in the oil fields and would come back and forth on weekends. Us girls would run clear to the creek when we'd see him turn the bend coming home. But the oil fields finally dried up and we had to depend on farming for Uncle Joe. He'd been begging my daddy to do that for a long time, and my daddy loved Uncle Joe and he loved my daddy. And we had these big grown boys to work and Uncle Joe thought we'd make good renters. Well, we begin to be poor when my daddy stopped working. He was no farmer. Actually, he loved having a watermelon patch and would plow on Momma's garden and raise interesting little garden stuff. But the hard work in the corn fields started falling mostly to the boys. I think Papa was a weakly man, and Uncle Joe always said he never had a well day in his life. He liked to fish and hunt and trap.

"And we begin to be poor. Seems like it was flash floods. We were living at the fork of Gladie Creek and Klaber Holler which had a branch big enough for good-sized fish. One flood in June washed all our great big garden off. It was too late to plant again, and that's the only time the government helped us. They declared us a disaster, I guess, and sent two or three bushels of soy beans we could eat, or sow and raise for hay to sell. The big June tide in the Twenties ruined about all the river people close to us. Then another flash flood started in the night, and the cattle and horses were fastened in the barn by a small creek. Seems like it drowned them all. It's been so long ago I can't actually remember how it really was. I know the whole thing made us so poor that we never caught up. A few years later the boys begin to leave home. I can see it. They drifted away as soon as possible because there was nothing for them there but food and shelter and they had to work like dogs to get that.

"Then Christmas became things Momma could buy at the secondhand store in Pine Ridge, usually cut-out paper dolls or a box of used crayons. Mostly it was an apple and an orange apiece and some striped candy. They'd have a pretty good size poke and you'd get more than one piece. We'd hang up the stocking, and they always tried to have a big stick of nickel candy in each and then the little odds and ends they'd picked up at the secondhand store. And they always tried to have firecrackers—I don't believe a Christmas would pass but the boys didn't at least get that. It's like people do now on the Fourth of July.

"And Momma always made some kind of attempt at Christmas dinner. Usually saved a chicken to bake and always tried to have the dried apple stack cake made with molasses, but sometimes she didn't even have spices that was supposed to go in them. Poor old thing. I don't know how she did it. And how she climbed those mountains and cliffs, nearly always great big with child. Either she'd just had a baby or was carrying one. But she never stopped working. She wasn't a pampering woman. Nobody got petted but the baby. And the next year there'd be another one, and then the one born before would be taken over by the next oldest children.

"So Daddy and Momma grieved at Christmas. I heard them. I laid awake and couldn't sleep. I heard them talk about how things had come down, how it once was and how it was now. How bad they felt about not being able to put hardly nothing in the stockings. But us children were tickled to death. We couldn't go to sleep for excitement, even knowing it wasn't going to be anymore than that."

Lily May hesitates, her hands still moving with her words. "See, people just had to make do with what they could get. There was always so much work to do—ground to clear, and rocks to pile, brush to burn, plowing and planting to do, and we planted by hand, you know, somebody coming along behind covering. On the hillsides which were nearly too steep to be plowed, you had to chop the weeds out with hoes, and it'd take the whole family to do that. Then came corn gathering time.

"But before that, huckleberries would come in July and last about a month on top of all those big cliffs, and we sold them. Berry trucks would come along on old highway 15, picking up huckleberries from the different pickers. My brothers would carry the huckleberries four or five miles from the ridges to these trucks which came along every so often, and sell them for fifty cents a gallon. That was good money, and a big help for buying for fall and winter.

"Now, I haven't seen many huckleberries in the Gorge for thirty years or more. They seemed to disappear when the forest reserve come in. Forest fires used to burn those ridges off—they didn't have any berries the year they were burned, but the next year the huckleberries would come back thick and rank. The mountain would be simply blue with them. But when the forest reserve come in, they stopped all fires, and the huckleberries began to get scrappy and to disappear.

"So we sold huckleberries, canned and preserved them, and

made pie and cobbler. We also picked blackberries to sell, but they was only nine or ten cents a gallon in 1931 or '32. In the fall, I stayed in the woods picking pawpaws and persimmons. Through the summer there was wild raspberries and strawberries. Chimney Top was richer than any place for wild things to eat. Possum grapes usually grew around the creeks and river. They were real sour and seedy, but I kind of loved them. I don't believe Momma ever made jelly with them because it took so much sugar. Summer grapes grew much higher, on top of the mountains. They were dark blue, looked powdery on the outside, and got about the size of a cranberry when you'd find a good kind. We used those to make jelly and marmalade, and Momma'd strain the seeds out when she cooked them, thicken them a little and make a grape pie or cobbler. Make sweet dumplings in it—roll them out real flat and round and pretty with a glass. And summer grapes made the best wine, along with elderberries and blackberries.

"From 1932 till about 1936 there was also a good market for ferns in the Gorge. You cut them off low at the ground. We always took a coffee sack along, wet it, and filled it full. That would preserve them until we got to a fern truck. They'd always show up once a week at Nada or Slade, and they would buy all the ferns people would bring them. They'd usually haul them to Cincinnati or Louisville to sell them. Florists used them for background foliage and in flower baskets, and ferns were very popular in the Thirties. So we'd make a little money, usually about fifty cents a day and very seldom over seventy-five. We didn't go by bags, but we counted them—there'd be 200 to 300. Sometimes we'd walk for miles across them mountains where we knew they was a lot of big ferns. A certain kind would get two feet long. And these people wouldn't buy just any—they had to be big, green, and not broken.

"Another good source of money was ginseng. We'd dig it when the weather was too wet to work the crops. Momma would take ever single one of us little ones and my daddy'd go too, and she'd have us spread out in all directions. Momma was like an old sergeant the way she would run her family.

She'd holler every now and then, 'Are you watching for snakes? Don't get snake-bit!' And that way we would pretty well comb the territory. Today I think you get paid at least ninety to one hundred dollars a pound in some places for dried roots. But at that time it was about sixteen, seventeen dollars a pound and it'd take the whole family all summer to dig a pound or two. By the time you washed it real good and put it in the sun for several days—bringing it in at night and taking it back out—seemed like it would dry away to almost nothing. They were real fat, juicy roots.

"But sixteen dollars a pound! Two pounds of that was enough to buy our pencils and tablets for school, several bolts of goods to make clothes, and shoes for those who needed them, although we never did buy shoes. Just about the only cash we ever actually saw is what we got from ginseng and selling furs. All the stores bought things the river people had to sell. We'd usually just trade them in and never see any money at all. With it we got coffee and sugar, salt and soda, and coal oil for our lamps. But as far as groceries went, we raised everything we ate.

"Corn, of course, was the big crop. There was a grist mill at Nada run by the Mays family where we'd take it. Now I've hoed in ever little patch of ground in Parch Corn and up Swift Creek. Parch Corn, not Parched Corn, is the name of that area. I don't know how it got to be called that, but back when times were hard and mountain people couldn't get hold of coffee, they'd parch corn real brown, pound or grind it if they had anything to grind it on, and make coffee. I never tasted it, but I've parched many a skillet full of hard shell corn. Put in a little lard and salt, stir it until every kernel swells up and turns brown. Oh, it was delicious. We had an old hand mill and we'd even grind that plain old parch field corn and eat it with sugar and milk for cereal. The heat would make it brittle, and was almost like eating a potato chip—very crisp when cooked all the way through.

"Ever body around us lived much the same way. Now some owned their little places and prospered more than we did. They'd always carry biscuits with jam and butter, and ever once and a while some cake or things we never could have in our lunch pails, unless it was molasses cookies—what we called sweet cakes. But we couldn't keep enough flour for our big family. A lot of times we had corn bread for breakfast, made from our own corn that we'd take to the grist mill ever Saturday. We'd shell corn the night before and that was a party in itself.

"My dad and the boys would go to the corn crib, which was filled to the top on both sides, and they'd carry in two or three big sacks of corn after supper and the dishes was done. We'd all shell corn and save the cobs to burn. Momma always kept plenty of aprons for us to shell into, and the men would shell in a pan. Then the stories would be told, we'd talk over the day and the gossip that would drift back over the mountains from newspapers. We'd build a great fire in the fireplace and have a party. There'd probably be a bushel to a bushel and a half of corn to shell. We had a big meal sack of a real thick coarse linen, like towelling, and it seemed like that thing was six feet long! We'd shell it almost full, but leave plenty of space to straddle it across the saddle and put half on one side and half on the other.

"At first, before any of us got old enough, Momma would go to the mill. It took all day, and you gave the miller a peck of meal for payment. We'd always go to the store and post office each week in Nada, and that's where we'd usually get our meal ground. There's no post office there now. The mill was on down the creek from the old store, but they've been gone for years.

"So Momma took the corn until the oldest boys could, but it was hard to get them to go, Kelly especially. He was around fourteen or fifteen and was too proud of hisself. He'd been to Pike County visiting his relatives, and he got so he didn't want to fool with it. Then Joe took it over, then Custer. Of course, when they got to be teenage they left home for the mills, and Kelly went to the mines in Pike County.

"So us girls took it over. Momma wouldn't send one of us alone when we were young. Sis was fourteen and me about twelve. She would send us both, me on the great big mule we had named Ellen, and Sis on the old white work horse we had then. He was the nicest riding horse we had, and she was courting the miller boy, Wilgus Mays.

"I remember how she would go faster and I couldn't keep up, and going through the tunnel that old mule would invariably get over against the rock and try to rub me off! Skin my legs up—I've been so mad and hurt by her so many times! But Sis would run off and leave me, and she had on a white rayon waist and skirt she always wore when we went to the mill. I can see her on that old white horse, her blouse just a shaking in the wind, and me urging that mule, trying to get her to catch up. I'm the one who had the turn of meal—that's what we called this long sack of corn across the saddle. I rode on top of it, and we'd leave enough slack for me to sit on! Well, Sis would get there first, and her and the others would laugh at me, seeing my mule coming away back behind and the sack sticking straight out, it was so full. Of course, Sis would stay around the grist mill and talk to Wilgus.

"Coming back one time, the old mule went to loping, the meal became unbalanced and fell off, and I fell off with it. Well, I didn't know what to do. Sis was long gone across the mountain. So I led the mule to a high dirt bank, dragged the meal over, pushed it up just a little at a time till I got it on top of the bank, and then my mule run off. Then I had to catch her, bring her back, try to get the turn balanced across the saddle again, and by the time I got home I had a little bit of meal on one side and a whole lot on the other, and everybody laughing at me!

"On the slow horses and mules we had, it took around two hours to go from Chimney Top to the mill, and we'd be there for a time. We knew two or three families in Nada and we'd visit them or they would stop us to ask about the river people. Then once and a while someone would offer us a dinner, so we'd be gone most of the day. We also went to the secondhand store at Pine Ridge three or four times a year to buy clothing and whatever else we could find. It also sold groceries. That was a much longer trip and we had to walk up a steep mountain and lead the horse. They had a grist mill there, but we didn't use it because your turn of meal would fall off when you led the horse back down the mountain.

"Before the corn would get hard enough to take to the mill, we'd usually grit for two or three weeks. Several of the poorer families gritted. Some who owned their little pieces of land and didn't have to share with a landlord was able to keep enough corn to go to the mill all summer and buy flour too, and always have biscuits for breakfast. We didn't always have them, though we tried to as much as we could. We'd fry salt pork or side meat and make gravy to sop our biscuits in. Our hams we never did eat. We cured and sold them. We ate the shoulders and side meat, the jowls, but the hams we felt we just could not afford.

"The word would be 'grating,' I guess. But we had a grater or gritter Daddy'd make. He'd take a board about a yard long and ten inches wide. He'd tear up a little tin lard bucket and lay it on the ground, drive it just full of nail holes. Then he'd hammer the tin to the board, with the rough side out. You'd just rub an ear of corn up and down the gritter and it would come out in a coarse meal. Ever once and a while a whole grain would drop in, and Momma didn't have any sifter. Maybe she'd pick out a few grains, but usually she'd just bake the bread with all of them in it! If she had buttermilk she'd use that, and salt, and if she had baking powder or soda which we didn't always have, she'd put some in. Maybe she'd use an egg if we had them, but we took most of our eggs to the store to trade for other things we had to have. So we didn't have eggs often at home, and when we did it was usually one a piece.

"And we gritted bread. We hated to grit worse than anything! It took a long time to produce enough for that big family—a dish pan about two foot wide and eight inches deep, I'd say. And Momma'd bake it in long black bread pans. I guess they'd been tin and had built over the years until they got thickish. We hated to grit and we hated to eat it. But we were just so poor that we carried gritted bread to school and tried not to let others see us, the ones who had good biscuits with fried ham in between. So we were always glad when the corn got hard enough we could start to the mill and have big corn shellings. The boys'd get out in the yard and have a cob fight in the night and cold, dodging and hiding behind the house and barn!

"The corn shellings, of course, would start in the fall at corn gathering time. You couldn't gather it to store while it still had any milk. Saturday was always mill day because it was the only time the miller worked all day and the mill would be wide open from daylight till dark. So we'd have the shelling parties on Friday nights. It'd usually just be our family, but once in a while somebody from way across Pinch-Em Tight Ridge would come three or four miles, carrying a lantern, to get in on it with us and have a chance to visit. They had to go to the mill the next day, too. They'd tell what little gossip they'd picked up from the outside world, talk about their illnesses and rheumatism. They'd bring their guns and hunt on the way home. Their dogs would always fight with ours, so there'd be two or three dog fights. And it was all fun.

"Sometimes someone would bring a musical instrument if they had one, but there just wasn't any except in one particular case. An old man and his boy lived way across several mountains on Tarr Ridge. They brought their fiddle and banjo, and I heard three instruments playing together for the first time. And I can't tell you! Before that, Daddy just played the fiddle, and I felt a rhythm in me of some kind, but it was never carried out in my hearing. But when the banjo played along with the fiddles, I began to feel something I'd never really felt before—a rhythm in music. And oh my goodness! Now I don't know if we shelled corn that night or not!

"Actually, I think they were on a long walking trip and stopped to break the night. People often did that. Momma understood. She'd get up, even if they came after we got to bed. People'd always draw up their horses if they was riding, or if they were walking they'd stop at the fence and holler hello. My daddy'd get out of bed first, because we didn't know who it might be. Sometimes the voice would be familiar, a relative we hadn't seen in a long time, and we'd all get out. When Daddy'd see who it was and say, 'Get down and come in,' the first thing Momma'd do was kindle a fire in the stove and fix them something to eat. She was very hospitable.

"We took in strangers only occasionally. A few people would drift in who wanted to survey land, and a few were hunting for John Swift's silver mine. It's supposed to be buried in the Gorge. Somewhere in those cliffs he had a lot of gold and stuff. Then he went blind. Perhaps he was a pirate! I don't know! But anyway, somewhere in the Swift Creek or Sky Bridge area he had sealed it back in a cave, and they've been digging for years. And ever once and a while a digger would come through, usually an educated person. He'd come by with his pack and camping equipment in the day time. Momma would go to cooking and fix him a big dinner, and he'd give her a dollar and all us children a nickel a piece. Boy, how happy we were when somebody like that came around! For a nickel I could buy a box of crayons, and that's what I was always looking for. I'd also use colored clay rocks I'd find along the creek, where they'd been dampened and washed until they were soft. I could get several colors ranging from pink to dark Indian red, then blue slate, and almost black. On every big rock and every barn around I drew pictures with those rocks when I couldn't get hold of crayons, and my daddy quarrelled a little about it."

An astute observer, Lily May also uses her voice to fine tune what she is describing, shifting easily from wistfulness to guffaws to flat finality. Now her tone slips into a curious blend of schoolmarm fastidiousness and mirth. She is still a handsome woman, careful about her appearance, peppery hair still full and smooth. And despite her many remembrances and her long career in old-time music, she doesn't live in the past.

"I'll have to tell you this," she continues. "The corn crib was empty in the summer, and Sis and me built a playhouse in one of its sides. We carried all our corn cob dolls, little old pieces of goods, broken dishes and bottles, took flat rocks and boards and fixed up tables and chairs. Well, Sis had a fiery temper, and one day in the playhouse we got into a fuss and pulled a little hair. Both of us started running home, and of course Sis got there first as always, to tell Daddy and Momma on us. Then they let me tell my part. My daddy made a great ceremony of our punishment.

"He said, 'Now both you girls come here, right close to me.'

It was out in the back yard. Then he said, 'Now Charlotte, you and Lily May face one another, close. Now put your toes together, touching. Now Lily May, you put your right arm around her neck. Now your left arm.' He made Sis do the same. Then he said, 'Good and tight. Now, Charlotte, you kiss your sister. And Lily May, you kiss your sister—on both sides of the face.' Boy, I wanted to bite a piece out of her! And she did me, too! That was the most memorable punishment I ever got, and I don't remember him ever doing it again."

Lily May pauses for a moment, suddenly serious. "Lord, what a family, what times we did have." Then she smiles. "Momma had all her children at home. Grandma Ledford lived long enough to deliver me and Coyen and the little girl born between us. That baby didn't live even twenty-four hours, just time enough to be named Edna. I can remember because I went back to the breast after she was born. Momma was trying to get her breasts dried up and she got me to nurse some of it out. Boy, I went back to the breast and just aggravated her to death! She had to wean me all over again. I was two-and-a-half-years old, and she had to hire me to quit. She boiled me an egg a day—I was crazy about them and that done it. But the things she done before, of blackening her breast with soot. I was big enough to unbutton her blouse and get to 'my' breast, and when it was all black, I got so mad and hurt I went to the kitchen, got me a soapy rag and washed it!

"I got so jealous again when Coyen was born. We had a hired man who stayed with us a while, and he had me petted and spoiled. He'd get me on his knee and say, 'Now what are we going to do with the baby? Throw it in the creek?' He'd say things like that and I'd go along until he come to doing something bad. Then I'd kind of back off and he'd laugh—he knew. He was teasing, but he'd say, 'I'll tell you what we'll do. Let's stick him way back under the floor of the house.' And I'd say, 'No, he'll freeze to death!' And he'd say, 'Well, we'll put him under where the fireplace is and he'll keep warm, and you won't have to put up with him.' And he suggested all sorts of things to see what I'd say. But Coyen turned out to be my best pal, my best playmate, because Sis didn't care about music or

rambling in the hills and hunting like me. Coyen did. We just
laid out and had to be hollered at. Sometimes we'd catch old
milk cows and ride them. Momma'd be hunting us, and we'd
hide up in the trees, eating mulberries like birds, and knowing
we was going to get a whipping when she found us. And boy,
she was a sharp one. She hardly ever failed to find out what
we'd been up to. She was a keen judge of people, another
thing that helped us get into trouble with her a lot. She could
size up what we done before we done it!

"Sis always stuck close to Momma and the house, and
helped Pearl. Now Pearl was old enough to understand about
having babies and they let her work in the house and help
Grandma, Aunt Mat, and my Daddy—he was also talented in
that way and could assist. They had acquired big doctor books
that were handed down, I imagine—thick, well-worn books—
and they knew what to do in emergencies. There were supposed to be a lot of midwives in our background before
Grandma's time, and they seemed very much in demand. But
they hardly ever got any pay except a bushel of potatoes or two
gallons of sorghum molasses—they well knew the people on
the river who lived up these creeks and on top of the ridges
had no money.

"When the time come for the baby, us children were sent to
the woods or to my Aunt Dora's house way down the river.
Then one of the older boys, or Pearl or my daddy, would come
after us and say, 'Guess what! You've got a new brother at
home.' It was always a new brother, you know, one born right
after the other. Only four of the fourteen children were girls.
Of course Edna died, and then there's Rosa Charlotte, and
Susy—that's what we called her later. Black-Eyed Susan's real
name was Minnie Melina, after her aunt Minnie.

"Did I ever tell you how I got my name? Grandma named
me after one of her daughters, my aunt Lily May, whom I
never saw. She died of the flu epidemic during World War I.
She and her husband had not been speaking for a long time.
They did that in the old days—never divorced or separated
because of such big families, especially my people. So they
hadn't been speaking, maybe for weeks, but both were down

with this flu—him at one end of the house and her at the other. They died on the same day. And the day they died, they both got up and left their beds and met, still not speaking. He went and got in her bed, and she went and got in his, and they died. That's Aunt Lily May and her husband Charlie. They were probably in their late twenties or early thirties and they had such a big family, their children were eventually put in an orphan's home."

Lily May falls silent again, but she can't remain serious for long. She says, "But you want to hear about my music, don't you? How many times have we sat here and talked about it!" She laughs her deep "ha-ha" and sits square and dignified against her chair, a woman innately aristocratic, yet unpretentious in character.

She tells of a career begun in the early radio days of country music. Beyond the slow wall of the mountains surrounding her childhood, World War I ground to a halt and the Twenties began to roar. While crowds shimmied to jazz, a quieter yet quite large segment of the population yearned for the simpler days of the past—and its music. Scenting a counter trend, promoters scouted the Appalachian hills for songs and musicians to satisfy this nostalgia. It was during this period that radio started reaching the general public, and largely through its influence the isolation of mountain life began to disappear while traditional mountain music, then often referred to as "hillbilly" music, gained a wider audience. One of the most powerful radio stations in the United States, WLS in Chicago, started broadcasting "The National Barn Dance" in 1924, followed the next year by "The Grand Ole Opry" out of Nashville. Commercial country music was growing, and not even the Depression could smother it completely. And it was at WLS where Lily May broke into radio.

"Let me tell you about the first real instrument I owned. I had made me a bow. Things drifted back into the mountains from other places, and somewhere I'd gotten hold of a thin rubber string from an inner tube. I tied it to each end of a green willow stick, and I was going to shoot targets with it, using sticks for arrows. I sat down to rest way up on a hillside, and begin to pluck on that string, and it made a nice 'boing' sound, you know. Then I held it in my mouth, so I could pick and hold it and kind of anchor it. But I found when I moved my mouth, it would make a different tone and sound. So I commenced trying to play it, and before long I could do a whole tune on that thing. I knew my brothers, who teased us girls a lot anyhow, would laugh if I took it home, so I hid it under a ledge and would go back to it the next day and get away from Momma. It lasted quite a long time, until we moved on down the river.

"When I was about twelve, we left Chimney Top and moved to Bernie Finch's land. And we were still sharecropping about the same way. One day I was picking greens by the river and a little boy came down the road. This was around 1929, and a car couldn't get through then, just horses and wagons. This boy was swinging a fiddle by its neck and hitting weeds with it. Now to me that fiddle was a sacred thing, like something alive.

"I was already playing a five-string. I started on those when I was about seven. My brothers would make a banjo with hickory wood and ground hog hide, and order strings from Montgomery Ward. They'd dare us little girls to bother that banjo and hang it clear to the top of the roof. When they'd have to go to the fields to work, I'd get me a table and put a chair on it, get that banjo down and play until I thought it was about time for them to come home. So I learned quite a bit. But my brothers would go to the mines up in Pike County and take it with them. My daddy had played the fiddle so beautifully, but his got bursted falling off a wagon. And I just had been wild for a fiddle and those tunes were running around in my head till I couldn't do any good in school—when I got to go. So we'd been out of fiddles for three years, and I decided I had to have the one that little boy had.

"We hadn't lived long in that part of the Gorge and I didn't know him, so I asked where he was going and his name, and he told me. And I asked him where was he going with that fiddle?

"He said, 'I was just going home. I've been to my uncle's and he give it to me.'

"I said, 'Would you sell it?'

"And he said, 'Why yeah, I can't play. I ain't going to do nothing with it except trade it off.'

"I said, 'Well, will you go home with me now and I'll see if I can find some things to trade you for it?' I found an old flashlight with no batteries, a little sweater belonged to one of my brothers, and my precious box of crayons—I drew and colored too, and they were very hard to come by. And I traded all those three things there. That's the only things I remember, but I'm sure I hunted him up a lot more. He was happy, and oh Lord, that was one of the happiest days of my life. I believe it was fate, because I never heard of or saw that boy again.

"So I went to work on that old fiddle. It didn't have nothing on it, no strings and keys or apron. I whittled that out myself. I made the apron rough cut and I don't remember how I fastened it onto the end of the fiddle, but I believe there was a little knob I wired it on. And then I burnt holes in it to hold the strings with a red hot wire like I'd seen my daddy do. And then I whittled my keys.

"Momma quarreled all day trying to get me to work and I somehow managed to get away from her, because I was not going to let that day go by without getting my fiddle rigged up! So finally I got everything I needed. I found some blue sticky mud and filled in the cracks on it. We had some old scraps of banjo strings around the house that I strung it with. Then I made me a bow out of a green willow stick and tied some of our old white horse's tail on it. His name was Charlie and he was just as dirty as he could be. The boys were always teasing him and had him kind of mean. They'd blow in his ear and pull his tail, and he'd bite and squeal at them. I was still small and hadn't ridden him much, and I was afraid of him. Well, I found him in the barn, with his backside pointed right at me. I climbed in a cow stall first, reached over with a pair of scissors, and chopped me out a big hunk of his tail. He kicked a little and swung his head around at me, but he didn't bite. So I tied each end of the hair to the stick and drew it tight. Then it was shaped like a bow that you could shoot with an arrow! Of course, old Charlie's tail was dirty and greasy and I had to have some rosin, so I found some oozing out of a pine stump and I rosinned my bow with that. Last I put a rattlesnake rattle inside the fiddle to improve the sound. All mountain fiddlers did that to pick up the tone quality.

"And Momma was watching all this and getting more worried than ever. She liked for all of us to work. She loved my daddy's music, but now she got awful aggravated when us kids took it up and wanted to play all the time. There were so many chores to do. So I slipped off from Momma and took my fiddle and went away-way up a mountainside and behind a great big boulder, hoping she couldn't hear me. I didn't want to hear her either. And I stayed up there the rest of the day. I knew how to tune one—that was all in my head. And those songs were all in my head. I learned to play about three that first day: 'Callahan,' 'My Horses Ain't Hungry,' and 'Old Joe Clark' or 'Sourwood Mountain'—I've forgotten which one. But anyway, I was in business.

"You know, grandaddy had a story about that first song, 'Callahan.' There was a man by the name of Callahan who had killed somebody and was to be hung. My great-grandfather was going to the hanging. My grandad was about nine years old, and he said he cried and begged until his daddy took him along.

"When they brought this man out to be hung, they asked him if he had anything he wanted to say, and he said, 'Why, yes. Somebody go get me my fiddle.' He had his fiddle in the jail. They brought it to him and he set down on the edge of his coffin—they always kept a old big rough pine box right there on the premises—and he played his tune. Then he said, 'That tune I made up when I was in jail, and no other son-of-a-bitch will play it but me.' And when he said that, he raised his fiddle and bursted it over the edge of the coffin. Somebody in the crowd was supposed to have remembered the tune and played it, and named it 'Callahan.' But I've since heard that tune played in other places—it was a different tune, but told exactly the same story, so I begin to doubt there was any truth in what grandad said.

"Anyway, that's how I got started playing. See, I heard my

daddy play every night. As I've said, that's something we'd do—pop corn or parch corn, and he'd play his fiddle tunes. He also played the autoharp till he traded it off to a kinsman. But he couldn't sing. He had no more than a half octave range, and he'd strain to reach notes that wouldn't have been hard for anybody else. His voice would pop into a yodel, and we'd go to laughing and he'd get mad.

"We got more from Momma, songs like 'Barbara Allen' and 'Pretty Polly' and some of those primitive ballads. Her people were hard-shell Baptists and string music wasn't allowed in her house—it was of the Devil and so on. So any ballads she learned she had to slip in and hide. She had quite a few. She sung in a high-pitched voice and off-key a lot, really had no music in her, but she did love my daddy's fiddling. She thought it was all right for him and the older boys to sing, but was unladylike for us girls. Of course, we learned them eventually from the boys.

"And now when I started to play, poor old Momma fussed all the time, but she couldn't hardly get a lick of work out of me until that old fiddle fell apart—which was in a couple of years.

"With all those tunes running so clear through my head all the time, I wasn't worth a dime at home or at school. I just felt that was keeping me from what I wanted to do. Once when I brought home such a bad report, one of my teachers said, 'She's absent-minded, she's just that absent-minded.' Well, I had never heard the term before and when I heard my parents talking about it that night at the supper table, I thought it meant—I kind of knew what 'absent' meant—but I thought it meant I had no mind. It was gone! That woman liked to ruin my life in an innocent way.

"But on down the river, I went to school to Ruby Mays—her people were the ones who had the grist mill in Nada, and they were real friendly and a little bit musical. And Ruby had a guitar. Well, she decided to make something out of me. I don't know why she thought I was smart enough to learn, because as I say no other teacher had found me that way. She began to take me home with her, and I'd ride with her on horseback.

She lived over on the highway six or seven miles away. I'd go home with her on the weekend, every Friday for a while, and she would play her guitar and sing and teach me songs and chords. Then she'd talk about her boy friends or just anything like I was her equal. Then all at once, before I knew what hit me, she'd have me working at arithmetic and subjects I was weak in. And somehow—I believe it was to please her—I begin to come out of it, because there was going to be a school fair that fall. She was determined that I was going to be there and win first place. Now whatever inspired that woman to think, knowing how slow I was in the work, that I could ever do anything first place in school, I don't know. But anyway, she'd go home with me, spend the night a lot of times, and we'd work. But we always had our music first, and I believe it served me and my friend in music and made me want to please her. I won second place in the county as the best all-round scholar and my parents couldn't believe it. I couldn't believe it either, and it seemed so easy to do. But if it hadn't been for Ruby Mays, I never would have done it.

"One time an uncle brought us a trunk of books he'd accumulated, and my daddy got as educated as any professor! He was kind of like me—you couldn't get no work from him either! It was his books and the fiddle, the fiddle and his books. Poor thing. At that time he had no fiddle except for the one I'd patched up, and he was too dignified to take hold of what I'd rigged up for a bow. I don't remember him even trying a tune on that, but he was proud because I was doing it. He got so educated out of them books—him and Momma both! And finally us kids found things there to read. My father had a lovely writing hand too.

"Once my old fiddle fell apart, somehow my daddy got enough money to order a new one. It was seven dollars from Sears and Roebuck. My little brother Coyen had been trying to play my old fiddle, and with the new one he begin catching up and passing me in no time at all. He was a highly accomplished fiddler at the age of twelve. But both of us played the fiddling contests. See, bands from out of Lexington radio would play Stanton ever once and a while, and there was always plenty of friends on the other side of the mountain that had cars and would take us to play these contests. Sometimes my brother'd win it, and sometimes I would. But a trick thing I did would usually take it away from him because it was judged on applause. I'd play my regular tunes, maybe 'Mocking Bird' and 'Cacklin Hen,' then I'd go out—I kept a pair of new overalls for the occasion—I'd put them on over top my dress. Then I'd come back and play 'Pop Goes the Weasel.' Where you pluck the strings twice and don't have to use the bow, you can change the fiddle into different positions. Well, I'd play it through first the regular way, then I'd play it in back of my head, then in back of my neck and behind my back and behind my knees. I'd put the fiddle bow between my knees and rub the fiddle up and down on it, and then on the 'pluck-pluck,' I'd take it back up into position. Then I'd sit on the floor, fall back, and play under one knee, and then the other, then under both of them, keeping my knees raised. Then I'd bow up a little and play under my back. When I'd hit the floor and finish my tune, of course they'd tear the house down. That way I'd win the contest, which was unfair as it could be, because it was Coyen that won on purely good fiddling. I was about fifteen or sixteen. I didn't let Momma know I was doing that, because she wouldn't have approved at all! I guess word got back to her, but she done found she couldn't beat me and she had to let me go—course by that time she'd decided I wouldn't amount to nothing! I'd always been called the laziest one in the whole family, and I know it was my music that caused it.

"So Coyen and I fought over that fiddle all the time like we had with our older brothers over the banjo. But we both got real strong on it, and we moved on down the river to Henry Skidmore's farm. This is still the Red River Gorge. I've lived all over it and hoed corn in almost every field, hillside, and little old patch of ground up and down that river, from Parch Corn all the way to Bowen—if not at home, then for other people. We'd work for others when we got our own crops laid by. They paid fifty cents a day, and the last I ever did, at the Skidmore's, they paid a dollar a day and boarded us, which was good

money. That was about two years before I got into radio. I
went to WLS in 1936.

"The Skidmores hired several people, including me and Sis,
and in two weeks we laid by that whole home farm. Their
mother, Mary, would cook the biggest dinner of home-made
cottage cheese, a big pot of beans, buttered beets, lettuce and
onions with boiled eggs in them, jam rolls with cinnamon
sauce over it for desert, and all the good buttermilk in the
world. We'd eat like working men. Then we'd help her with
the dishes and go to the front porch, get out the fiddle and
guitars, and have an hour of music. Then back to the fields.
We'd help her with supper and dishes, and the boys with
straining the milk. They sold cream, and had a cold-house and
a refrigerator run by gasoline. They'd save the cream and kept
up the road so a car could get in and someone could pick it up
once a week. We'd help them run the separator and wash the
parts, then go back to the front porch and play music until
they had to make us go to bed.

"Mary would fix a big pan of water for me and Sis to bathe
in, and put it in the diningroom where nobody could see us, for
privacy. The boys went swimming in the river and took soap
and towels. Us girls didn't have nothing to swim in. We'd sleep
in Mary's parlor and the boys slept upstairs. Her parlor had a
piano and flowered carpet, and in the front room where the
fireplace was, linoleum covered the floors. They were the
river's leading family in the lower Gorge. They commenced
owning farms just a short way from the tunnel where you
cross the bridge and turn left onto the River Road, and went
durn near to Bowen. There were a few other places in between, but they had the cream of the farms. Yet they worked
harder than dogs, especially those two oldest boys, Morgan
and Albert. Their daddy was crippled and they had to run and
manage the farms. The feeding and milking fell on them after
a whole day's work in the fields.

"So, my sister Rosie was getting hot on the guitar, and
that's something we'd never had until we moved down the
river to the Skidmore's. Mary had one and she could play
several chords and sing. And we went wild after that guitar.

Her son Morgan was real good on it, and Coyen was already sharp on the fiddle. I played the fiddle, banjo, and guitar, although I'd kind of quit the banjo. So the four of us got up a little band and called ourselves The Red River Ramblers! And we begin to be in great demand all up and down the river for square dances.

"Red River was highly social in that part where the lower valley widened out and there was a lot of farms and families and young people. They even had church going on in a little school house. Almost every weekend there'd be a square dance at different people's homes. The biggest deal would be when we had a working to go with the dance. The men would mostly set the tobacco or clear the ground, but if there was single boys, some of us grown girls would help too and just let the mothers cook the big dinner. They'd fix thirty or forty dishes, and whoever was having the working would furnish the party. The women would have a quilting frame somewhere and talk in the afternoon. Everybody'd knock off about four o'clock to go home and do the chores, get cleaned up, and then get back for the square dance. Some of the best river people would come and most had good riding horses. Of course, all we had was our work horse. Then some walked for miles to get there—wade the river and everything else. Word would be passed up and down the river, and musicians and others would come clear from Cane Creek and off the ridges. The dances would start about dusky dark and go on until the parents told us to quit, since mostly only young folk came."

Upon request, Lily May crosses the room for her banjo. As she lifts her Vega White Lady from its case, she smiles. "I didn't think you'd really let me get by without playing a little." Once she gets comfortable again and starts tuning, she decides to remove the resonator to muffle the banjo's loudness. She fools with the drone string, then swiping over the rest she sings "I Ain't Going to Work Tomorrow." When she plays, her eyes close with the expression of a child hovering over a birthday cake, ready to blow out the candles. Her movement is concentrated joy and involvement with the music. And whether she is performing for one person or a crowd, she finishes with a flourish.

After another song, she lays the banjo aside and picks up her story. "It was these square dances with the stringed music that scared Momma to death. She got it from her father, of course, that it was an idleness and therefore of the devil and the devil's workshop. She gradually let us go, if our brothers or Daddy would go with us. We'd take a lantern. Sometimes us girls have waded the river to our waists to get to somebody's house on the other side, and it might be winter time. We'd carry our shoes and take along a dry rag to wipe our feet off right before we got there, and put them back on. We made a lot of new friends and they took us right in because of our music.

"Momma also didn't want us going because there was always so much work to do. Her mind was running a mile ahead of everybody else's. She had it laid out in her head ever night before she went to sleep, how the next day would go and what everybody's job would be! She announced it at the breakfast table or sometimes before she went to bed, and my daddy'd agree with her. But she was the main leader. We could have prospered with her, I believe, if my daddy hadn't done so many foolish things. Oh lord, he traded us out of so much that we needed! Buddy, if he saw a gun he'd love to hunt with, he'd trade off the last milk cow we had. And poor old Momma, she just worried and fretted herself to death with his foolishness. Boy, she loved him, though, better than anything in this world, and she kind of had him for a pet, you know.

"So in her own way, she run things, and she'd whip us all for sassing. I remember once she slapped Sis. Momma said, 'Tonight we're going to shell beans, and I've got three or four bushels.'

"We said, 'No, now we can put that off until morning, Momma, cause tonight we're going to Rhett Garrett's house to square dance.' Rhett and English were like young people and they'd welcome us. Sometimes we'd even spend the night at Aunt Rhett's.

"Sis said, 'Momma, I'm twenty-one and we're going.'"

"Momma said, 'No, you're not.'"

"Sis, said, 'Oh yes, we are!' And Momma slapped the fire

out of her. Then she said, 'All right, so you're twenty-one and you're going. Them boys you know ain't interested in you. When they get interested in girls, they'll marry someone down at Stanton that's of their own standing. They're prosperous people, you are poor girls—your reputations are all you've got. So you're twenty-one and you're going. Well, Lily May's not a going.'"

"Sis said, 'Oh yes, she is! She's a riding with me.' Momma let us go, poor old thing. She was left with three little ones for the weekend again. I feel sorry when I think about all of it. But we didn't stay late. We went back and done the beans the next day. I remember that was the last time she went to whip one of us.

"We didn't get any church until we moved on down the river, except for experiences with our mother and daddy. They had a big Bible and read aloud from it a great deal, especially my father. And it seemed like they preached the fear of God more than the love of God. Momma and Daddy were both that way. My daddy's people were all Methodists. Several of his uncles were preachers or circuit riders. On my mother's side, they were hard-shell or primitive Baptists, and as I say they didn't allow stringed music in the house. That's why we had such a hard time when we all started playing! But I'll swear, I still believe the fiddle was one thing that attracted Momma to my daddy. She loved to hear him play and thought it perfectly all right, him and his fiddle. She never grew tired of hearing him. And she had a few old songs. She was so work minded, one of them was typical of her: (sings) 'We'll work till Jesus comes, we'll work till Jesus comes. . . .'

"I believe in her mind she thought manual labor and the work she was doing was what was being referred to in the song—that was the kind of work we was supposed to do, as God had laid it out for us.

"Yet God is supposed to be a god of love, and we needed more of that in the preaching, I believe. They could have said God will love you if you do this, or He'll crown you if you don't behave. There was too much hell fire in their teachings, especially Momma's. As I said, she'd lived in Pike County, and in those mines—gosh, ever thing in the world went on.

"I'll swear, I never knew much of what meanness was. There were a few mean families in our area, but some we never come in contact with. When we got grown and went down the river, they'd sometimes come into church and always raised a disturbance, was almost always drunk and would start a fight. One woman was supposed to have lured men to this cabin and charged them for her services. She seemed kindhearted and nice when you'd see her, but Momma kept us carefully away from her. They crashed a few of our square dances, and one of them who lived way out on a ridge was always drunk and waiting to cut somebody's throat. Now, ever body carried a gun when they went to a square dance, though they usually kept them concealed so we didn't know they had them. So there could be trouble sometimes, but this didn't happen very often.

"I'll never forget this. One night we tried to have a square dance and one of my uncles came in. Ever time he got drunk he thought he was a preacher, and he would climb up in a tree, preach, and go on so! And of course string music and dancing was the devil—you couldn't have it in your house. He was a man in his forties, and we hadn't seen him in a long time.

"He come in and said, 'What's going on here, White?'

"My daddy and momma was watching the little ones and sitting by the fireplace in the next room from where we were dancing. And Papa said, 'We had a working today so we're having a square dance tonight.'

"He said, 'Now I want that music stopped and these people out of here!'

"And my daddy said, 'Listen, it's none of your business what we do.'

"He said, 'By God, that's my sister, though, and I know how she was raised. And I'm not going to have it!'

"My daddy got down his gun and says, 'Oh yes, we will have it. And if you don't like it, you can leave here.'

"And boy, he got scared. He took off, and you could see that lantern running, absolutely flying through the cornfield the way he came! He lived first with one relative and then with another, aggravating people, renting and trying to run big farms by hisself, working like a dog and talking about how no one else would work. We all kind of dreaded him.

"There'd be a square dance nearly every Saturday night somewhere on the river, though seldom through the week. We'd sometimes have a little play party games on Wednesday nights. When they could finally find a preacher, we'd hold a prayer meeting on Wednesday night too, and that was used as a social thing as well as religious. So if we had anything extry at all, it would always be then, to break the week.

"A play party was 'Skip-to-my-Lou,' where you change partners and sing as you go through the figures. But you didn't use music and you didn't dance—it was more of a run-through: (sings to the tune of 'Skip-to-my-Lou')

> Hurry up, hurry up, this will never do;
> Hurry up, hurry up, this will never do. . . .

"And you go back and forward, make a circle and hold hands. And Momma permitted the kissing games—she was young. So we'd have those and play party for a while: 'Skip to my Lou,' 'Paw-paw Patch,' 'Swing a Lady Up and Down,' and everybody'd sing while you did the figures.

"We'd have these at one another's houses, whoever had a floor big enough to circle in and dance. Ever body had to do the evening chores, the milking and feeding, and then we'd go to gathering in about dark. Sometimes we'd quit around eleven o'clock, and at some places they danced all night. We'd just invite the closest families around, and we always made candy. There were some good cooks down at the river, and the boys brought the brown and white sugar we needed to go in it. Sometimes we'd have them buy Karo Syrup to make peanut butter roll, and they would have to go to Bowen or Nada to get it.

"So ever body'd be in the kitchen, watching us daub it out. Some nights we made pull candy and poured it into shallow, buttered plates. Boys and girls would pull together on that taffy, then swap ends till it got real hard and pretty. They'd kind of court a bit, team up and pull together, and I found myself pulling by myself most of the time! Then we'd stretch the candy out and let it lay for just a minute, then take scissors and cut it into little pillows. We'd eat it all up that night.

"We'd usually play a while first, because ever body wanted in on the candy and we didn't start making it till later. So one of the more forward ones would say, 'Now let's Skip-to-my-Lou,' and we'd go through that till we got tired of it. We'd waltz around, and sometimes the boys would line up on one side and the girls on the other. A girl would come out of the corner for 'Swing A Lady Up and Down'—it was like 'The Virginia Reel,' and we'd sing to accompany it. Then we'd make candy and eat it.

"In a kissing game like 'Snap,' only four was up on the floor till they'd all kissed. They went through some formations first, then they'd put their arms across one another's shoulders, all lean in and kiss their partner, then the opposite partner, and then their own again. Then they'd break up and leave one to choose the next three. When we'd get tired somebody'd say, 'Now let's play Spin the Bottle or Spin the Plate,' and whichever one was spinning would kiss whoever it landed in front of or pointed to. A thimble brought on post office kissing. I've forgotten how 'Who's Got the Thimble' went. Maybe they'd pass another little object around—gravel or something. But two would have to go to a dark room and kiss, then they'd come out blushing, and we'd go through it again.

"The older people would always be there and join in, the kissing games and all! Course, they weren't old. To us they were, but I imagine that most were in their late thirties. So, down the river, most of them would join in, though some in the upper Gorge wouldn't—they were too bashful or straight-laced. And the young ones had to be brought along, but they'd set in the corner and be good. They didn't take part in the games—really, they were too busy fighting one another.

"A square dance to us was entirely different from one of these play parties. You had to have fiddles, guitars, and banjos. It was a lot bigger deal. We had a lot of play parties till we moved on down the river and they got to finding out about our music. I think it was hard for them to rake up musicians until then. The square dances, of course, attracted more people. A big play party had twelve people, but a crowd at a square dance was twenty-five. Word would be passed up and down, though we'd try to keep it amongst ourselves on the river. But if other people would hear and come from Cane Creek and off the ridges, once they got there they'd be welcome."

Lily May rubs her knees and chuckles, "You may not be able to tell it now, but I was a good dancer and won some contests square dancing, but all I really ever wanted was to play. My great thrill was me and Coyen on the fiddle and four or five guitars around us.

"Then every Sunday, since nobody else would go with me, I went by myself to Natural Bridge. That was about an eight mile walk from Red River. I'd start out around daylight with my fiddle in a flour sack to protect it, go across the mountain and walk up the railroad through the tunnel clear to Natural Bridge where an excursion train ran from Cincinnati every Sunday. They had a big pavilion built right by the track where the train stopped, and it had benches all around, a big dance floor, and a good roof. I'd sit there and start playing by myself, and there'd be a few workers wandering around. But soon crowds would start pouring out of the hollers. Poor old plow boys would come with their little pints of moonshine stuck down in their shirt, the shirt a bagging where it'd run down next to their belt. They'd always wear a long-billed cap or felt hat, and they'd stick a rose under each side of it. And they'd wear a white shirt and a pair of overalls or some kind of khaki work pants as their Sunday best. They'd come first.

"Then the excursion train would come and unload, well dressed people would get off, and they'd all start square dancing. By then several other musicians would appear and start helping me. I would sit in that one spot the whole blessed day and play the fiddle, and that's all in the world I wanted. I never thought about money or wanting to get up and dance, or getting me a drink of water or anything to eat—I had no money, of course, to eat on. So I'd play all day, and most of the other musicians would. Some of the old people that later made it in radio like Asa Martin—he'd come sometimes, and so would Shorty Hobbs, who made a fine mandolin player and comedian, and lived up in Wolfe County. I think Asy was already in radio a little bit and recording at that time, but not Shorty. Then Ruby Mays' uncles, Carl and Tom, would come with their fiddle and banjo, and we'd play and they'd dance all day.

"Somebody'd pass the hat, and we'd get ever thing in the world in it—a little money, it was all pennies and nickels and dimes—and bobbie pins, sticks of chewing gum. And pretty soon, all the old boys from around there would get drunk and go passing their caps and hats, and run off with the money! But I usually wound up with at least of couple of dollars every time I'd go. That was along when we had our Red River Ramblers."

Lily May's career might never have grown beyond the bluffs of the Gorge had she not caught the attention of another Kentuckian. John Lair, one of the first promoters to popularize the barn dance concept on radio, doubled as talent director and music librarian at WLS. He helped develop such stars as Red Foley, Merle Travis, and Homer and Jethro, and "discovered" Lily May at a talent contest, bringing her to Chicago in 1936. A man of shrewd business sense and foresight, coupled with an affection for and knowledge of country music, Lair ultimately envisioned his own barn dance transmitted from his native Renfro Valley. To this end he began assembling acts to take with him from WLS. One of his most original ideas centered around a string band with a unique drawing card—all women performers.

"Some of Morgan Skidmore's people came from Rochester, Indiana, to visit and they heard us. Our Red River Ramblers played for these people and one of the boys said, 'I'm going to take you all home with me if your parents will let you. I'm going to manage you and get you started in something. I know you're good enough.'

"Morgan's folks didn't mind. It was late fall and they had all their crops harvested. But we had an awful, awful time getting Momma to let us go. They had to come back and get us, but we finally went. We auditioned in radio at Fort Wayne and their friend, Mr. Kreighbaum, that had a theater in Rochester, put us on his stage for a week doing fifteen minute programs between movies. And we won every amateur contest around there. Well, Fort Wayne and Indianapolis wanted us, but they said they didn't pay salaries. We'd just have to get on and make it by selling song books or playing personal appearances. So we did until we was finally able to get an audition at WLS in Chicago. Now that took a lot of doing and a long wait because WLS was a 50,000 watt station heard all over the United States.

"We spent all winter with this Skidmore family in Rochester and finally the station manager and some big wigs listened to us. Something about us stirred them but they didn't know quite what, and they went and got Mr. John Lair. After listening to us, he talked for a long time and said, 'I can use Lily May, but it will be some time yet because I don't have the authority to get her on the station. But I've got plans later on in the spring where I believe I can.' Then he said, 'I can't use everybody, I'm sorry.' Coyen was too little and there was a child labor law against hiring him."

Today Lily May realizes John Lair already had the Coon Creek group in mind and two other girls lined up for it. At that time he didn't think her sister Rosie was a good enough guitarist for his purposes, though he later changed his mind. But without the rest of the Red River Ramblers, Lily May felt her confidence and ambition ebbing away.

"Really, I just wanted to play to suit myself and for square dances and friends," she says. "Well, anyway, the others went home to Kentucky and were deeply disappointed. I was deeply hurt too, because I never thought of us any other way but as a band together.

"Mr. Lair sent me back to the Skidmore's in Indiana and said, 'Stay there because I don't know when I'll call you.' Finally in the spring we got a letter saying, "I'm coming to Rockcastle County, Kentucky, my home, for a week's vacation. I'm bringing the program director here with me.' That's Mr. Lair writing that. He said, 'I can't hire you myself on the station, but if I can get Mr. Safford, our program director, and the station manager down here to hear you on stage and see how you go over, I know that they'll hire you.'

"That's exactly what did happen. It was a big talent show and they had people from everywhere. I first picked the guitar and played one of Jimmy Rogers' blue yodels. Then I took the fiddle, played 'Cacklin Hen' and just tore that house down. My little brother Coyen backed me up and I won first place. I couldn't believe it. Here come Mr. Safford, who pulled me off to one side and said, 'How about a contract with the station?' And somehow I was afraid of him. He had that clipped Yankee brogue I hadn't heard much of and a twitch in his face, and was a very nervous man. I was half-afraid to sign with him. I don't know why, because he turned out to be nice. But Mr. Lair then pulled me off to the other side and talked about a manager's contract. He had great plans for me—with him—and went a little more into detail about what kind of idea he had.

"He had the authority to put a program on the air up there and it was going to be Red Foley, the Girls of the Golden West, and me. He was going to call us the Pine Mountain Merry Makers and we'd have thirty minutes a day on the station. I'd also be on 'The National Barn Dance' and playing programs on the road where I'd be paid extra. I'd start at sixty dollars a week, which is like nine hundred now. That was in the Depression. I said, 'All right. I'll sign a contract with you, Mr. Lair, because I trust you. You're a Kentuckian, you talk a little more like we do, and yes, I'll be glad to do that.' So I gave my brother the prize money from the contest—two dollars.

"In a very few days Mr. Lair sent me a five year manager's contract and five dollars to help me on my way. Then some neighbor men were working on the River Road in the Gorge, trying to get it in shape for cars. I went down there to see if there was any work for me on that section. They laughed and said, 'Lily May, you can be water boy.' They was going to pay me fifty cents and I said, 'Oh, I don't want to do that. I want to dig ditches and pile rocks and earn a dollar and a half a day.' So they put me to work and I turned them off a good job for a week. And that gave me a little more money.

"My daddy sold a hog. He was tickled to death, he was so proud. But Lord, what a time we had with Momma! Aw, she had read these old magazines that drift back into the mountains. She'd heard stories where the young girls who went to cities were captured and sold into white slavery, beaten into submission and all kinds of things. And she was scared to death of cities and what could happen to young girls there. It was all right, I think, for her to be afraid. But she needn't have worried. I could watch just as close as she ever could. I was pretty sharp about knowing how to stay out of trouble.

"Some friends cleared out one of their houses and gave a big square dance in my honor and we almost danced all night. Then early the next day they took me to board the train at Winchester, about thirty-five miles from the Gorge, and we said goodbye. It was the last part of August and very, very hot. I had on my best outfit, which I was proud of—a gray flannel suit with a blue felt hat and shoes the Skidmores had bought me. And I begin to look around and see everybody so nicely dressed in cool clothes. I knew mine weren't right and I begin to worry about what would be thought of me when I got to WLS.

"I knew Scotty and Lulu Bell was there, and that year she was voted Radio Queen. And Uncle Ezra and the Hoosier Hotshots was there, the Prairie Ramblers and Patsy Montana—and they were all top acts. At that time there was a hundred performers at WLS, and it was known as the greatest hillbilly station on the map. So I begin to look around the train and feel an apprehension. But I had my fiddle in its case shaped like a coffin beside me, and I was already on my way. I was nineteen years old.

PART THREE

FURNACE MOUNTAIN STORIES

And so I came to Furnace Mountain, a place I'd never been. Yet I know the people, and they know me.

Pigeon Milk

Saphire Cotes: Furnace Mountain, 1980

You don't have to stay long in Furnace Mountain to figure out there are two kinds of people—the simple and the sly. It's as clear as day, I told Mommy. I was changing her bed. And I told Stanley when he got home. It's a downright shame what some people will do if they're not watched. He didn't want to hear. He just wanted dinner. But when I slapped the cobbler down beside him, he was listening harder.

Them Suttons have lied and wiggled their way around since they come to this country, I said. If they'd keep to fleecing them Winnebagos and Airstreams, nobody'd raise any dust about it. But Ida's a cousin to us, Stanley. Do you hear me!

Leave be, Saph, he said.

You're getting kind of choppy in them log woods, forgetting about kin, I said. He just pushed away from the table and went outside. I heard him plop in his chair on the porch . . . what he always does.

Now I married that man because he had some gumption. He had this place—saved, paid, and paved—right on the main road. That's what in those days I called a man and incentive. I cleared the table and checked on Mommy. She was already snoring in the back room. Then I went out on the porch. Stanley was still there, of course, smoking cigarettes and watching the cars on the road. Aurell and a few of his boys honked by.

I bet they're on the way to Winchester, getting supplies for the big weekend, I said. Seems like Carl's whiskey would be cheaper now gas is so high. Stanley kept smoking.

I guess they like to joy ride, I kept on saying. He'll never have nothing, that Aurell. He's not much of a man, if you want my opinion. The cherries from the cobbler started burning inside me. I looked down the road to Sutton's store. Now, Stanley, I said, I'm going to give you one more chance to behave yourself.

Stanley stubbed out his cigarette. Saph, you don't know what you're talking about. People make mistakes, even you.

This ain't a mistake. I'm telling you what the truth. Ida sent Carey Sue for two cans of pop. She gave a twenty from her government check. Carey Sue, she came back with two cans of pop, all right. And thirty cents change. If you think that's a mistake, Stanley, you're getting thick as tough mud in your old age. Stanley winced a little at *old age*. I was getting to him.

You don't know none of this yourself, Stanley fretted. You've only been to Sutton's once, when he opened last week.

I been there twice, I said, and that's two more times than I'll go again. I told you I thought a new store'd be nice in there. Save us a drive. But I ain't going to be fooled with like that. You can see for yourself everything in there's jacked up a quarter or more. And you know what he said when I asked him the meaning of it. He laughed and said, mountain surcharge. It warn't no laugh to me. I won't be winked over, least ways by a sly, citified cheat. I said to him, mountain surcharge, there ain't no such thing. Highway robbery is what it is. And then I walked out. That store's not for folks here. He's hurried in for the summer trade and when it's gone, he's gone.

That's once, Stanley said.

I tried to keep calm. Don't you listen to me? I told you already I was there today. Carey Sue didn't know a thing was wrong. I happened to ask what she did this morning. Then I had the sense to check Ida's purse. Carey Sue started crying, bless its little bones. She thought I was mad at her. Well, I took her back over there. This time the trouble was with Sutton's boy. I explained what happened, and that boy just sat there, squinting behind his glasses. I think he's on dope or something, Stanley. He said he didn't know nothing about it. I asked him, I said how can you lie in this child's face? He snapped on a radio behind the counter and turned it up real loud. When I wouldn't go away he said, Lady, you're nuts.

No, I said, I'm a Cotes, Miz Stanley Cotes. You remember that.

Carey Sue was crying again, so I took her home. And I stopped by Idy's—that purse is just about empty.

Stanley shook his head, then raised his fingers to his lips, almost like he was still smoking. Saph, there's no way Ida should be living by herself. You know she ain't been all there for a long, long time. Most likely she lost the money, or Carey Sue did.

Ida can't help the way she is, or that she's got no close kin that cares, I said. We've all got our weaknesses, Stanley. The truth is you've always been ashamed of her.

I belched and tasted sour cherries. It was true Ida'd never been quite right, when you get down to it. But that's not what got Stanley. No. Stanley will never get over how Ida took to her bed. One day she started speaking in tongues, took out her teeth, laid down, and never got up again if she could help it. And Stanley's jealous of anybody but himself getting to laze around, sick or not.

I added, Blessed are the poor in mind, for *they* shall receive rest, Stanley, not you.

Don't start that again, he said. There's no sense talking to you these days either. You need out of this house. What about a visit to Jimmy?

And what about Mommy? I said. Who's to tend to her—feed her and turn her in the bed a dozen times a day, wash her and empty the bed pans? You?

I could try, Stanley said, quietlike. I could tell he was serious, because he finally looked at me. I was so mad I couldn't see straight. It wasn't right of him to sneak Jimmy into it—he knew better than to suggest such a thing.

So that's all your good job means to you, I said. No way the foreman's going to let you traipse off and then have you back at your own sweet time.

He's a good man. He'll understand. And besides, he owes

me a favor or two, Stanley added. You think about it, honey. You've done nothing but wait on Mommy for a solid year. And Ida, too, when you can. Everybody knows the goodness you done. Maybe you need to get free for a while.

I guess that's what you do in the log woods—get free, doing favors and such, I said. He'd not mentioned any favors to me. He don't do any favors for me.

Stanley patted my arm and said, You think about it. Then he watched the road again. Thursday and already cars piling through. Weekends are bad in fine weather, but throw in Memorial Day or a Fourth of July and everybody from Louisville to Cincinnati wants up the ridge to the National Forest and what they call the Gorge. What they find so fun about a three-day traffic jam, even in them hills, is a God's great mystery. Every year it gets worse. Thousands a stopping up everything. Sutton'll make a killing at his store, and Stanley— he gets a charge too. Don't you Stanley?

Don't I what? Stanley said. He looked at me like I'd gone simple.

You gawk as much as them, I said, pointing out a dune buggy with five kids hanging on. They waved at us.

At least it's social, Saph. Stanley didn't even see me when he said it. He was too busy checking out the dune buggy. Now I can tell when a man wants left alone. I went inside and turned on the tv. The news was just starting. Nothing but refugees and hostages, hostages and refugees. I'm sick of it. Either put up or shut up is what I always say. I switched to the Winchester station. The weather girl was pinning a sun over Kentucky when I heard the porch creak.

Where are you going, Stanley?

Out of cigs, he called back.

Stanley, don't you dare to do that! I pushed out of my chair. Stanley was already half way across the road and heading for Sutton's. We eat the same, but somehow Stanley stays thin. It don't seem fair. I caught up with him, though. I was breathing hard, but I did it. A camper was pulling in for gas and got in his way.

If you set foot in there, Stanley, you better mean business, or my name ain't Saphire Amelia.

Aw, Saph, is all Stanley said and walked in. You can bet I was right behind him. It was Sutton's boy still working the counter, if you can call it working. He was slinked on a stool, picking at his hand with a safety pin.

You never saw such a one-room dump. Marshmallows stuck behind brillo pads, them pre-fab sandwiches poking around the Ale Eights, sun tan lotion with the milk. Who-knows-what-all stuffed in boxes. And like I say, everything expensive. Tourists may not know better, but there's others that do.

Hurry up, Stanley said. Get what you need and let's go. It's hot in here.

I don't want nothing from a dump like this, I drawled out real loud. The boy acted like he didn't hear. A man was paying for gas and talking to him. We got in line. The man was holding a credit card. I don't think the boy even looked. No credit, he said, and kept picking his hand. The man fumbled for some bills and a map.

Look, he said, does this road go to Crazy Creek camp grounds in the park or not?

The boy never said a word till he finished making change. His hands seemed to ooze around the money and he kept the cash box closed so tight I couldn't tell if he give the right change or not.

There ain't no park, the boy said. He looked like a lizard, sunning himself on that stool.

The man jammed the change in his pocket and said, Impossible. It says here on the map this whole big area is the Daniel Boone National Forest.

That ain't a park, the boy said.

The man jerked the map away and slammed out. Stanley moved toward the counter.

Stanley, I said, I guess when you got the only store in five miles and smack on the road to the *park*, you don't give nothing away but nastiness. The boy blinked behind his glasses, but didn't say a word. I know his type.

Salem Lights, Stanley said.

Is that all? the boy asked. Stanley nodded.

I said, I changed my mind. I do want something. I want

some duds. I know you got those. Duds, the boy repeated. I pointed at the candy behind him.

You mean Milk Duds, he said.

Say, you must have gone to school somewheres, I said. Now throw me a Vienna sausage on top and you go to the head of your class.

The boy got them and clicked on a little calculator. $2.89, he said.

I hope you people get a register where folks can see what you ring, or your business is going to end up like the funeral trade—dead. I said that while Stanley paid. The boy just shrugged and sat back. He knew better. He didn't bag our stuff, though. Stanley picked it up and turned away.

Stanley, I said, low but loud enough. He sighed and faced the counter.

You Sutton's boy? he said.

The boy kind of simmered on his stool, pure meanness on a stick.

I hear his name is Jasper, I said.

Is your daddy around, Jasper? Stanley asked.

He ain't back from Leaco yet, the boy allowed, sullen-like.

I couldn't believe Stanley. He said, Leaco. We got a boy ourselves lives in Leaco. He grinned and glanced at me. Got him a good factory job. Jimmy writes us all about it.

The boy just let that lie there. He warn't no fool.

Still smiling, Stanley said, Well, and he stroked his chin with his free hand. Then he said, turning—Just tell your daddy I'll catch him another time—and he headed for the door. I stood and watched him go.

The boy looked me over and said, You forget something, Miz Cotes . . .

Not what you think, I said.

When I got home, I just had Stanley give me the change and I counted it again. Then he set down in front of the tv. Pretty soon he was asleep. His head sagged sideways and his mouth was hanging open—a way to crik your neck but good. I left him set and went to bed. If he won't consider kin, why should kin consider him?

Around three, Mommy begin hollering for her pills. She's always afraid I'll forget them. I never do, but that don't make a difference. I try not to lose my temper with her at night. Her hands grip thin cold on mine when I hold the glass. Sometimes she can hardly pull the water through that hospital straw.

Aw, honey, thank you, she said. Can you rub my feet a little? I can't feel them no more.

I did, and she quieted down. In the front room the tv was humming test patterns. I switched it off. Stanley was still asleep in the horsehair chair. Now to somebody else, Stanley'd have looked real plain, all slumped over like he was. But not to me. I like Stanley best when he's asleep. I can get a good look at him then. I moved up close. The logging had toughened him. A man can still be a lot of a man, even if he is pushing sixty. Stanley's face was brown like his work shirt. Wrinkled like it too, but not much. I felt along his shoulder, satisfied. Yes, fleshy and hard as a boy half his age—what I like. I shook him.

Come to bed, Sugar, where you belong, I said. Stanley's mouth shut and his eyes half-opened. I know a happy man when I see one. I turned out the light and felt my way to our room. I could hear Stanley stumbling behind me. I lay back on the bed and waited for him. In some ways, I've never had complaints about Stanley. No complaints at all.

Before six I was up. I swear, pretty soon I'm going to need a hoist and line to get my legs over the side of the bed. A body should never get old. And if they has to get old, they sure shouldn't get fat. Fat is what I am. Ain't no way around it in the morning anymore.

I got dressed and tried not to make too much noise. Even Mommy was asleep. I got the bucket and went outside. I stopped at the privy and then at the well. You know, chores seem light of a summer morning. Everything smells nice, night still around but heading out fast. Dew on the honeysuckle and wild peppermint by the well. The lid was not quite straight. Darn that Stanley. If we get a snake or something dead in there, that's our water spoiled. When I lifted the lid, warm air hit my face so gentle. The click of the chain and the bucket sloshing down. Rust on my hands, wet. I'm going to get me a new chain next week for sure. And some cement to fix the crack in the well box. When Stanley gets paid, watch out, well. I'm going to start on you.

I lugged back to the kitchen, lit the stove and put on the kettle. Then I went to wake up Stanley. I shoved him around a little and said, Get a move on. You need an extry early start this morning. The road's going to have lots of traffic later. No, don't you go curling back with that pillow. Breakfast is ready, smoking hot and good.

Of course, it warn't ready, but it would be by the time Stanley got there. Every morning of our married life I have fixed that man eggs and homemade biscuits with sorghum, or preserves in these later years. Coffee, bacon too if he wanted. A man's got to have something to draw on during the day. Stanley never was one of them poor fellers having to pat their belly and say, that bread sure is getting thin in there. No sir. I keep up my end of things. I always have and I always will. Even Jimmy got the same when he was here for it. I did right by him and loved him the best I could—nobody can say different and be telling the truth. And he should have done the same. But you know, sometimes I believe you're damned if you do care and damned if you don't.

Stanley clumped to the table and ate. He don't talk of a morning, which suits me down to the ground. I don't have time for foolishness. I fixed his lunch fast. When he wanted his second cup of coffee I said, No, Stanley. You get out of here. I told you I have a lot to do. He didn't like it much, but he went to the bucket in the sink, dribbled water on his face, and wiped dry on a sleeve. He didn't try to primp like he sometimes does. After all, it's no beauty contest in the woods, or it better not be.

Here's your lunch, I said. The river fog's breaking early

today. It's going to heat up out there. You be careful. We can't afford a stroke of no description.

He left.

I was glad. I had a lot to do.

It couldn't have been much past noon when I heard the pick-up on the drive. What's Stanley doing back? I said to Mommy. I had her propped out of bed for the first time in three weeks. I was right impressed till she started sniffing about breakfast. Didn't want no egg, no nothing. Just coffee and a piece of that ratty-looking whole wheat toast she likes to dip in it.

Maybe it's the mailman, Mommy said.

Now, Mommy, I said, you know Frank don't come till around three. And he don't drive a pick-up.

Maybe we'll get a letter from Jimmy today, Mommy said.

Don't hold your breath, I said, turning away.

Oh, Mommy moaned, I think I might die today, I feel so poorly.

I said, Suit yourself. Ain't nobody stopping you.

Sweet Jesus on the cross. When she starts whining, there ain't no other way to be. If you baby an old-timer they'll go simple on you. Like poor pitiful Idy. Old and alone—all gone simple.

When I got to the kitchen, Stanley was breezing through the door. If you've been fired, I said, you can just turn around.

Stanley didn't pay no mind. He said, We ain't worked an hour or more when the foreman let us off. The holiday, I guess. I'd have been home sooner but the road was clogged. And if them Angels didn't gun me off the road—there must have been twenty or thirty cycles.

Yeah, I heard them go by here. They must have stopped at Sutton's for gas or whatever people like them eats, I said, moving toward the sink.

Why Saph, Stanley said, the dishes ain't done.

I said, Stanley, when did a mess turn your face? You forget some people's had their hands full today, slaving. I got Mommy setting up, cleaned the bed, give her a bath, powdered her feet and cut her nails, fed her and the chickens both, hunted up the eggs—more than you could ever think of.

I tried to keep my face straight. I wanted to see how long it would take him to catch on to my little trick.

I didn't mean nothing, Stanley said, I'm just surprised. He hung around the table while I cleared it.

Why are you so touchy today? Stanley asked.

I just heated water for the dishes and kept quiet—why I don't know. Long ago I learned the silent treatment don't work on Stanley.

What about some lunch, Stanley said, his lips starting to pucker.

I made you lunch already, I said. If it'll do for the log woods, it'll do for being underfoot here.

I ate it, Stanley said. I got hungry, stuck in that road jam.

Well, there warn't nothing for it but to fix him some more. I said, baloney and cold cobbler will have to do.

Stanley had finished off two sandwiches and was scraping crust from the pan when Aurell come in.

Knock, knock, Aurell said.

If you bring in them flies that buddy up with you, you better not leave them when you go, I said from the sink. That Aurell. He didn't even stop.

You been over to Sutton's today? Aurell said, his beard bobbing with excitement and stained with tobacco juice.

No, Stanley said. Saph, give Aurell some ice tea.

I poured it.

Aurell said, Somebody's took paint and wrote big on the side of the store *Memorial Weekend Special: mountain pigeon milk for sale.*

Pigeon milk, Stanley said, that's crazy. Pigeons don't give milk. There ain't no such thing.

I could tell Stanley was thinking. His eyes were blinking real hard. That's pretty funny, he said.

What's funnier, Aurell said, is Sutton. The store's crammed with folks. When me and the boys saw the sign and another down the road, we got curious like everybody else. We went in. Every one of them damn tourists was asking for that authenticated pigeon milk, bugging Sutton, searching the shelves, kids knocking stuff on the floor. I guess his boy's painted the sign over by now. But Sutton, he didn't like it at all. Me and the boys just cracked—pigeon milk for sale.

Maybe that's what he got so late in Leaco last night, I said and snickered. Stanley was starting to look at me.

Aurell giggled through that lumpy face of his. He said, Yeah, well, it serves him right. I hear he's a slick from Covington somewheres. We don't need his kind of truck around here.

Him or his boy, neither, I said.

Saph . . . Stanley started.

Now, Stanley, I said, cutting him off. If you're the man I know you to be, you'll go back over there with Aurell and you'll want the pigeon milk like everybody else. You'll say, Why I hear your boy was selling it, two cans for $19.70. You ask your boy if he didn't sell some to Ida Stoke's five-year-old girl friend for that price. Then, Stanley, you finish up with: course, I wouldn't know about it myself. I'm just sorry you run out. It must have been awful tasty to cost that much.

You! Stanley said.

Aurell began choking on his chew, laughing so hard. Really, he looked disgusting. Now Stanley, he's not much of the joke kind. But even he laughed, short and fast, holding his poor full belly.

Aurell wiped his face and said, Saph, you're a wonder woman.

Yeah, Stanley said, she's a good old thing. He looked like he was going to reach over and peck my cheek.

Aw, Stanley, I said, not now. I got work to do. And so do you, across the road. I turned back to the dishes. I'll swear, why men need such incentive to act right is a God's great mystery. I'm telling you the truth.

The Equality

Aw, honey, is it you? . . . It's so kind for you to come. Please, here, sit on the bed—I can't hardly see no more. . . . . It's been especial lonely since Saphire took sick. . . . Well, honey, they don't know anything more—just it's her heart. I told her she was doing too much, but she never listens to me. You know Saph.

And how's Bud keeping? . . . . And your ma and pa? . . . . Do they think she'll have to have it out? . . . . . . Oh, Lord, I never thought I'd live to see times like these. Honey, your arm's so thin—are you eating right yourself? . . . Yeah, Stanley's fine, bless his soul. He's doing the very best a man can do without his wife. It's awful hard with Saph gone. We was hoping to get her home for Christmas, but it don't look good now. Honey, don't ever wish for no children. You worry yourself to death about them. I worry more about other people than I do myself. . . . What? . . . Yes, if I live to the 29th of December I'll be 104 years old. That's a long time, ain't it. . . .

Yes, Bowen, what we called Filson then. But Mamma and Dad lived in so many places, it's hard to say where I grew up. When I was ten, we took a team and covered wagon to school. I remember that. It had double beds and we thought we was flying in it. That was the last schooling I had. We moved back to Bowen in a year or so. I think Dad must have been poorly, even then. So we come back, and I married Charlie. . . .

Honey, I didn't know you remembered him so clear, all these many years Charlie's been dead. You must have been real small. . . . Really? . . . Well, I declare. I'd forgot about that. . . . I met him when I was just a little girl too, before we went to Illinois. I didn't know who he was, but I thought I loved him, though he was eight years older than me. . . . Honey, I was fourteen when we got married. Ain't you glad you didn't do that? . . . Well, that was the ways in them days. But I almost had to run away all the same. Mamma, she had nine children and I was the oldest girl. She wanted me at home to watch the little ones and do the chores. But I made me a dress anyways. I got a sheet and made the prettiest thing—white muslin with a ribbon tie in back. Mamma kept me so busy I didn't hardly have time to fool with it, but I got it done finally. Aw, I wish you could have seen it—it was so white and full and clean.

On the day I got married, I hoed corn till dinnertime. Then I come to the house for a bite and got ready. Mamma never looked up from her churning, not even when I put on my dress. Oh my, it was pretty, but she wouldn't say nothing. And when Charlie come, she wouldn't speak to him neither. It was awful. . . . No, she never said a word till we got back from the preacher's house. Charlie was carrying my things to the wagon. Mamma followed me as far as the porch and then tapped me on the arm. Law, her mouth was set like it'd been starched and ironed on her face. I'll never forget it. She pinched me and said, Now you get back here on Wednesday. As you well know, that's the day I wash and you take care of the babies. I won't have no fooling around.

Charlie, he come back and took my other arm. That's the only time I ever saw him pure red in the face. He said, No, she'll not! She's my wife now, and she'll not be coming back here to do the chores. You've nearly worked her to death. Well, no more.

I was so proud of him. He stood there, that blond hair shining in the hot sun, so proud in his black meeting suit. He took hold of me and pulled me loose. And Mamma had to let go. She laughed once, harsh like, but I didn't care. Charlie helped me up into the wagon. I remember sitting there and just wanting to drive on forever. Honey, don't ever be scared to be happy. When it visits you, take it in, and don't listen to nobody.

He passed on at 88. . . . Still, he was a handsome man even then. I thought he was the handsomest man in the world. And the kindest. I wanted to go with him then, too, but I guess I decided to live as long as the good Lord wants me to. . . . All told I had eleven children, including your grandpa Bud. They're all dead now but him and Saphire—she was the youngest. I had her when I was forty-one. Now my first baby came—let me see. We got married and moved to the river in 1890, and it was not real long after that. Miz Lucie Hern from the Calaboose country come and delivered him, but it just lived two years and two days. He took the summer complaint. The doctor just folded his hands and prayed—that's all he could do. . . . Babies'd take the diarrhea and wouldn't eat nothing, wouldn't nurse. You don't hardly hear of it now, do you. . . . Poor little Jamie. He never had a chance at nothing. And another one, he died of the flux. About four of them died small. We took them to Bowen where my dad was buried, and Mamma and later Charlie. They've all been there for a long, long while. They're all gone. . . . Honey, if you was to live to be 104—I'm not 104 yet, but I'm getting a way up on it. . . . Yeah, I *would* like some water, if you don't mind. I ain't talked so much in a long time, what with Saphire Amelia gone. Most likely, you've heard it all before anyways. . . . I can't get out of bed. I just have to lay here. . . . Is it time for my pills yet? . . . Five o'clock—yeah, that's all right. . . . They're on the dresser. . . . . Thank you, honey, I feel better now. . . . No, that's plenty. . . . . . You don't have to go yet, do you? I'd be pleased to have you set a spell. . . .

Will your dad get off for Christmas? . . . . Oh, I want so bad to see him and Bud. Do you think they'll come see me? . . . Tell them the old saying—time waits for no man. Bud knows that, but you tell him again. I miss him so bad, and all of you. Time don't move when you have to just lay here. . . . Is it cold? . . .

I'm sorry. If you throw a little coal in the stove there, it'll warm up fast. . . . . Thank you, honey. . . . No, I got plenty of quilts on. . . . Do you like this one? . . . . Then why don't you take it. I made it for Josiah's wedding, but he got killed before they could marry. Remember hearing about that? . . . Well, I'd kindly like if you would take it. It's just old. . . . Yes, I'm sure. I'm right proud you want it. . . .

Honey, we come over to the river after Charlie and me got married. I thought it was the awfullest place I ever seen in my life. There wasn't nothing here but some old shanties. The bottoms looked all right—they had a few spaces cleared for planting. But everything else was growed up around and looked awful. Them hills looked awful. I didn't like a town, but where the country was level and pretty. There wasn't no train yet—that little dinky hadn't even been built, I don't think. . . . Yes, I had a filly I rode sometimes. But once I was riding through some pine brush, where they'd cut timber and it had all this thick foliage. I heard a awful noise in there and when I got to the cliffs, a wildcat was standing there. It'd been following me and tried to head me off in that narrow place. Finally my dog chased it, but I can tell you it scared me to death. I stayed right close to home after that. . . . Well, we was shantying there, raising corn, and Charlie was logging with his brother, Tom. You've heard me talk about him. He was living over by the Jewell Rock then. They were logging with a yoke of oxen and when they'd start up steep places, them cattle'd fall on their knees and bawl. . . . No, Charlie wouldn't hit them. He'd just raise his whip and they'd start to beller. I could hardly keep from crying if I heard them, it was so pitiful. One time we had a big snow in May and the next morning the drifts was so deep it had broke the young timber down. The ice hung so thick they had to cut the cattle out of there. . . .

What, honey? . . . Well, we lived in what we called a little old shanty, what I was telling you. You don't see houses now like they was then. It was just a little plank thing of a couple of rooms. They looked awful, but people stayed in them. We lived way back on Swiss Creek, I guess a mile. Law, you couldn't hardly tie anybody up in a place like that now. When we first moved in, nobody was there but us. There wasn't hardly homes at all, not even here at the Furnace, or anywhere much on East Fork. And the few that come around was like us. We raised a good corn crop by the river, and there wasn't anything to feed it to—just a few hogs. But we was happy. We was living on our own, away from our folks. And back up in there, about everybody was on the equality—nobody had nothing. In a while another family moved right in above our place. Had a log house, of one room. I still remember Miz Larson right well, though she died of the cancer not long after they'd come. Oh, it just ate her up. And all she could do was lay there and take it—lay behind them rough, dark logs in that little speck of no place. I'd go visit and sit on the bed and hold her hand, just like you're doing to me now. I didn't have no children then. I thought I had plenty of time. We'd pray together. Her face was wrinkled like leaves on the ground, and turned the color of dead leaves before the end. Sometimes she could only whisper, and sometimes it wouldn't be her at all—just the corn shucks crinkling under her. But when she was dying, she tried to tell her family—Now when you move out of here, I want you to take me with you—it made me cry to hear her. But she's a laying there still. She wanted them to dig her up and not leave her. They didn't. . . . I guess all them Larsons are dead and gone now too. . . .

I remember one day Charlie took a yoke of cattle and went to trade at Bowen for a wagon-load of stuff, enough to do us for a long spell. Menfolks would only go then, you know. I forget if he stuck at the river ford or what, but he didn't get back that night. So I was staying there alone. Oh, that holler was like a fist, all closed up tight and hard. It was so dark, you couldn't see your hand in front of your face—it was like you was already in the ground. And I studied about poor Miz Larson laying in her grave, and nobody else around for miles and miles. She couldn't hurt me, but it made me sad to think of her. . . . I guess the poor old thing never had a flower on her grave in all this time. . . . .

No, honey, I'm all right. . . . Yes, turn on the lamp if you want. I can't hardly see and I forget. . . . Stanley should soon be here. Sometimes he gets held up, but he comes home most nights, sooner or later. . . . Aw, you don't have to stay. Ain't nothing can happen to me no more. Now you go on. . . . You'll stay? Bless your soul, you're so sweet. . . . No, don't worry about supper. You've got your own to fix for when you get back. Maybe Stanley'll see to it later, if he gets home. Just sit here by me and rest yourself. . . . Honey, if I was starving I couldn't see to cook. I must look like the wheels of bad luck. I feel like the hind wheels of something. I sure want to go to a better place than this world, don't you? . . . Heaven to obtain and burning hell to shun—I've always heard that. . . . Sometimes I do very well. I try to be helpful to Stanley, especial now that Saphire's gone. But most days I just lay in the bed. There ain't nobody here. . . . When a person lives to get old, they ain't no good, are they. . . . I guess the Lord's got some purpose to let me live so long, don't you think? . . . Aw, honey, I don't know. When I was young like you, I never thought nothing about getting old. But if we live, we all get old. And then, honey, when we can, we all have to die.

The Luck of Elmer White

The Nada Tunnel: constructed ca. 1911

My name is Elmer White. You don't know me, but you should.
If you've ever ridden the log train from Nada to Furnace
Mountain, you've gone through my handiwork. I guess I've
been a man of many talents and turned my hand to anything
that's come my way. You might say my greatest gift is smell-
ing out the right place at the right time. I'll be there. And I
know when not to be there—that's the trick, and the kind of
talent most needed to build a tunnel. Lots of times luck was all
we had to run on. When blasting is your main-line work, you'd
better have a barnful in your pocket. And I did.

When I was seventeen or eighteen, I left Slade for the coal
country. Drought was shriveling our garden back to dust, and
the South Fork of Red River was clogged thick and stinking.
Even the trees was losing their leaves. The locusts was shed-
ding and looked scabby. One morning I got up and walked the
field—the beans was strings of ash on the cane poles, the corn
was twigs and scorched brown, the tobacco was wilting down,
and come housing time there wouldn't be nothing to cut. I
could see it all very clear.

So I hit the road before the worst heat of the day. Pa shook
my hand, then give me a hug. He looked embarrassed, but did
it fast anyway. His arms felt brittle around me. I reached over
and kissed Momma. She was crying into her apron, and had
more water on her face than had rained all summer. I felt
better once this leave-taking was behind me—figured most

likely they were relieved to see me go, didn't need me underfoot no more. When the road burned hot and fine under
me, I just pulled my hat down against the sun.

So I called on Uncle Ezra Ledner down in Pike County. I'd
never seen him before, but we must have been close enough
kin, because he passed me on to a friend that run a mine or
two. The friend looked me over. He had thin lips, and they
wrinkled up like bacon frying when he laughed. He tipped
back his hat and said, You ain't fit for much but pulling pillars.

I didn't say nothing—I needed the job too bad.

He said, You can do that if you want.

I looked at him level and said, You just got yourself a hand,
and a better one than you think.

He said, Maybe. But it's too bad you ain't a orphan boy—I'd
rest better if you was.

He laughed his little laugh again, and turned me over to my
new partner, a guy more mole than man. His name was Willy,
but everybody called him Shakes. I could see why. When I put
my hand out to him, his fingers jerked and sweated against
mine and his eyes twitched, especially when he looked toward
the boss, like he was doing now. But he was a nice feller as it
turned out. Nice, but not lucky—it was on this first public
work that I come to know the difference.

You'd understand better if you knew what pulling pillars
meant. They'd mine coal in rooms about forty feet apart under
the ridge, and them slate ceilings would be held up by these
little fence post affairs somebody must have called pillars for a
joke. Well, you mine under there for so long, the mountain
grows right heavy—ain't nothing holding it up but those
spindly posts. Now when the miners would see those pillars
start to bend and hear the splinters pop, they'd hurry right out,
you can bet.

That's when I'd get sent in. Yeah! That was my job, and me
an absolute greenhorn. Me and Willy'd take sledge hammers,
jerk out the spikes and take up the tracks as fast as we could.
The boss didn't want no equipment buried. Just as quick as
that room caved in, and it could be mighty quick, we'd start in
right behind, digging and laying the same track another way,

over and over. I tell you, I'd take the palsy I was scared so bad. They'd wave us in, and I'd start to shake, just like Willy, but I did it and made $1.50 a day. I was rolling in the money. Around harvest time I quit—I knew when I was ahead. When I got home, there was hardly no crops to come in, but my whole family was able to hang on till spring on what I'd saved. Nobody had to tell me that I was a man.

So the next year I went back. Willy wasn't working—by then he was more stump than man or mole either one. His legs had been crushed like wood pulp in a roof fall. I visited him once, and he started crying when I asked if I could help some way. Now that he'd been planted in one place for good, at least he'd stopped shaking. His wife folded the money in her apron when I give it to her and never said a word, and I didn't stay long, especially after she gave me a secret, nasty look—I could see Willy'd never had much luck.

This time the boss put me to working different. Now I could have lived with pulling pillars, but not with loading coal. The seam was only four feet tall, and I'd be bent over all day. You try shovelling coal into cars for ten hours and not straightening up once. Then you'll find out like me that you ain't a miner. Them that grew up in the pits, you'd always see them walking leaned over, like trees after a bad storm. They'd thump me on the back and say, You'll get used to it, and it won't bother you no more.

And I said, I'll be dead before I do.

I quit, and come back to Slade before summer was hardly started. That year I didn't end up doing much except farming and just ginning around the place. It was all right, and I helped put away a good crop. But I wanted better. I knew my luck was hot again when I run into Winter Jackson at the store up by Boling Branch. Winter was as wild a man in some ways as you'd ever admit to meeting. Believe me, I ought to know— we sure could cut it up and have fun. He was a fine hunk of shoulder and neck, and had eyes the color of slate. I was taller, but glad to call him friend. Picking a fight with him would have been like lingering too long under that mountain—I figured the effects would be the same. He wasn't too many years older than me, but his hair was turning white and shaggy as a sheep. You can bet I never let him forget it, when he was in a good mood.

I'd say, You must be drinking what you're making.

And he'd laugh.

And I'd say, No woman in these parts is going to look twice at a man both gray and broke.

And he'd laugh. But when he didn't laugh, I left it alone, and I never said such things around other people.

So I walked into the store and there he was, handling a fifty pound lard can the way a woman picks up a thimble. He saw me and tossed it my way. Elmer, he shouted, Why, where you been?

I lugged it back at him, end over end, and told him my story.

He said, I can't tell you mine, least ways not now, he added, looking around and grinning, more at himself than at me. I'm heading past Nada. They're going to build a tunnel in that mountain and run a logging train through. You hear about that? The timber's drawing them in there, and they're going to need help. Well, you know me, I'm not put off by making good money, he said, giving the lard can a thump.

I said, Opportunity don't need to knock twice on me either.

Next day I walked to Nada and signed up. Blasting paid the best, so I talked my way into that job. I'd never done it before, but I knew I could—in those Pike County mines, they'd drill and shoot, and I'd asked and learned. It was all in my head, and I knew my hands would do what I told them.

In a couple of weeks we started the grade up the mountain, and the boss put eight men under me. We'd drill and shoot and did right well. But when we got started on the tunnel itself, we stuck, and it wasn't our fault. The company went broke. So me and Winter decided to have ourselves a time. I knew a couple of fine ladies that stayed just outside of Clay City, and it became awful hard to keep checking every few days about work. We just forgot about it for a while. Then we heard another contractor had taken over and we got back on the job—good thing, because I was just about wore out.

Now, the first couple of shots in that tunnel was put in

wrong. You go look on the Nady-side today and see if it's crooked. I didn't have nothing to do with it, and I won't take the blame. I followed where the engineer put the stakes. The new boss, he called us both up. The engineer was a light weight they'd brought in from Lexington, almost as young as me, and had a face as thin as a fuse. He slapped his papers together and accused me of blasting wrong. When I told my side, he laughed short and kind of breathless-like, then said, I think I know where I put my own stakes.

He flung open a blueprint and said to the boss, I can understand why you have the men you do working for you. You have mules from the local farms working hard and long too. But these men, they have no training. They don't understand even the basic, the most obvious—look here—surely you see. . . .

He and the boss huddled together. I didn't know the new foreman either, but I did know that I didn't like the way they was talking—bent over so close, almost cuddled up.

I took off my hat. Wait a minute, I said. A mule's a pretty smart thing. He knows all he needs to for his job. And he does it good, too, if he's used right. And me—I know the basics of my job and a lot more. And what I don't know, I can make up myself and get by. I've lived here all life, that's true, so I know a mountain when I see one, a stake when I see one, and a fool when I see one. The engineer turned red and looked at the boss again. The boss thrust out his fat lower lip, but let it go. He needed me too. Later he allowed somebody'd tampered with the stakes to damage the company. I don't know where the truth lies. I just do my job, if people will let me.

So as I say, I did nearly all the shooting. Me and Winter put in the biggest shot ever set off in that country. We strung the hole first till we got it about thirty feet deep. Then we loaded in four cases of dynamite. When that blew, the face of the mountain jumped off into the holler. Oh, it was wonderful! Winter laughed and yelled, That ain't *dynamite*—that's what *Dinah-did* last Saturday night! He always said that after a shot, and I thought it was pretty funny, at least at first.

We started rolling the heading, and got about twenty feet

back in the mountain and them steam drills started melting us down. The sandstone was crumbling and clogging the drills, and gritting into our eyes. When we'd reset the drills, the steam would try and boil the skin off our arms. The sand was crawling over us and I felt blisters on my face. I could hardly see Winter, and him working right beside me. Wasn't nothing to breathe but that furnace fog of steam. So we walked out. I said to the foreman, You get air or we quit. He sputtered like one of those machines, but three days later air drills were hauled in, and after that I liked the job.

We worked past Christmas, a twenty-five man crew on each side of the mountain. If it had been limestone and hard, we could have finished by then, but the sandstone slowed us down. We was lucky in other ways, though—until February we had mostly an open winter. Then come weeks of dead cold and the boss hired a boy to thaw the dynamite. I watched him for a while and could see he didn't know what he was doing. I told some of the others, but the boy was related somewhere along the line to Winter and he didn't like having him thrown out of work. You know, Winter was like most big men I've known—he seemed to want peace over anything, especially among his kin and friends, which was lucky for people smaller than him. But sometmes I'd get awful put out, like now. All he'd do was shrug and say, Why Elmer, you keep fussing like this, you're going to turn into a little old lady—and gray like me. Well, I decided to let it ride, for Winter's sake.

But a few days later the boy's daddy come to see me at the company boarding house where the men were staying. This boarding house sat on the tunnel-side of Nada, or Lombard as we called it then. It was a two-story job as long as a barn, the bunks wasn't bad, didn't cost much, and I'd live there during the week, then hit home on Fridays or, like I've said, good-time it somewheres. On Sundays, people'd hold church there and a crowd would come in, so I didn't come back till night.

The dining room ran the length of the house and had two or three stoves fired up all the time to feed the men. I was still drinking my coffee when a stranger stopped Joe Jenkins, then headed my way. I knew who it was the minute he stepped inside. He looked like his boy, but washed out and thinner—a dirty, snow-bank of a man, you might say. I'd bet he was bald, but he didn't take off his hat. And he didn't put out his hand.

I'm Charlie Huntsman, he said as he stopped by my table, and I hear you been bad-mouthing my boy.

I said, That ain't true.

He said, He's a good boy, a game worker, and his boss ain't had no other complaints. Why don't you stick your nose out?

I understood how he felt, and I didn't get mad. Instead, I sipped my coffee and asked, What's your line of work?

He looked surprised and said, I was logging out them hills up the river before you was born.

Good, I said, Then you know dynamite. You can't watch your boy and say he knows a thing on this earth about using it. I've tried to tell him, and he don't listen or learn.

The man stepped closer. I put down my cup and got up. I never raised a racket unless it was brought to me, and I never swung at an old man, but then I wasn't going to let a logger chop me down, either.

He said, My boy knows plenty. I taught him good, and he's worked all up the river, at Wolfpen and Chimley Top special. He needs this job. It's his first public works and ain't nobody going to wheedle him out of it.

Buddy, I said, He's your boy. I think he's a nice feller. But I don't want nobody blowed up, and I kindly like this world. If he's leaving it, I don't plan to go with him.

The man melted back a little, but he wasn't really hearing me—just like his boy. He said, I'll talk to him, all right? I'll talk to him! But I know he's doing fine. I've learned him plenty. Then he bundled his coat tighter and left. I thought, There goes another lucky man, if that's all he knows about blasting— nothing but luck could have kept him in one piece.

Next day I complained to the boss direct. He listened but didn't say much. People shouldn't take me wrong on this—I liked the boy, and I didn't have a thing against them Huntsmans. Even the boss—he wasn't a bad sort himself. He'd put in a solid day's work like the rest of us. But neither him or the boy, or lots of others on that job knew what they really needed to know. And worse, they didn't have no luck.

A few evenings later I was the last man at the table. I always wanted my coffee first, if I didn't get slapped away from the pot. I like a mug and to just sit after a day's work and relax before I eat. The stoves clacked and sputtered, fired up and topped with food. The room would drift with good smells and smoke, a couple of hired girls laughing and scolding us to the tables. Iron kettles would be bubbling and clucking, grease popping—clatter of sticks, slam of fire boxes on the stoves, burn of corn bread in the skillets. They didn't set up the fancies, but there was always plenty. When I got around to eating, I'd scrape boiled beans and potatoes off my plate and try for seconds and thirds. More fat meat and biscuits. Now you can guess that Winter ate a lot—he spread over one end of the table and wouldn't let go till nothing was left but a grease slick. That night I ate even more than him, three times of molassy cake. By then all but Winter had left, and even he was looking disgusted. He didn't show no pity when I had to walk it off. He waved me away and said, I may not be much, but I ain't keeping company with a sow like you.

The second crew was trailing in as I was going out. They looked pinched up with the cold. I said, Don't you boys go ruining yourselves like me, tucking in too much at the table. Somebody cussed and nobody stopped. They was all trying to squeeze through the door at once.

It felt good walking through the clean, hard air. The sun had gone and the cold was drilling down toward zero. I wandered up the grade toward the tunnel, rock crunching under me. The trees and ridges was snarled against the sky, stuck and frozen stiff. The moon was gone, but the stars was drilling down too, hard and bright, driving spikes of frost. The night rolled out over the hills, hammered thin with ice. Oh, it was deadly cold, like breathing down metal. The tunnel mouth was wide and black and crumbling, ice frozen in bolts around it, the color of dead fish. A hole to nowhere—it didn't go nowhere yet. But it would. I'd make it.

I heard something, and not far off. I looked and saw a throw of light against the cliff. Someone was in the rock house up there and I went to see. On that little ledge of a cave was crammed the boy, his shepherd dog, a hustling fire, and five cases of dynamite.

I couldn't believe what I was seeing. It was like waking up with a hog rifle jammed against your face, or watching them pillars bend like hot wax under the mountain. All I could say was, What the hell are you doing?

He said, What does it look like? I ain't finished fixing this dynamite for the night.

Well, I said, I'm leaving here. But I couldn't move.

He said, ugly-like, There ain't no danger. I don't know what you got against me, but I don't like it.

His dog settled back at his feet, and for insult the boy threw a log on the flames. My eyes followed the log and suddenly I could move again. My luck was throwing me backwards. I shouted, Don't tell me there ain't no danger. That stuff's been froze and will go off!

I was running down the railroad grade, legs heavy with boots and cold, like wading through Red River terrible slow, or in a dream. Then the iron rails was ridged against my face and I couldn't hear nothing. The whole holler must have raised up and fell back. I couldn't think—I was just there. Then hands on me, turning me over. It was Winter, me in his arms. His mouth was moving, saying nothing, then—right, all right, be all right, you'll be all right. He held me a while till I coughed and tried to talk.

Winter laughed, give me a little shake, and set me on my feet. He said, Ain't nothing wrong with you but too much molassy cake.

Other men had gathered around and I started to feel a lot better, and then a lot worse, when we walked back to see what was left of the rock house. It's strange the way that dynamite did, hitting here but not there—like a storm, or like a woman trying to make up her mind. Just blind nature. The dog was still lying there just the same, only it was dead of course. But the boy, we scraped off what little of him was spattered across the ledge. That's all we could do. When we got back to the boarding house, some of the windows was broke, and even some of the dishes. Well, from that night on, everybody called me Lucky.

Next morning we found the rest of the boy scattered all over that holler, in bits not as big as your hand. A shoebox full is what we got. Winter give it to Charlie Huntsman when he come. I felt so bad that I couldn't look the man in the face. He just held the box like his life and said, Josiah. Nobody else said nothing. Winter walked beside his horse a long ways as he left.

It took almost a year and half to finish that tunnel, and nobody else got hurt bad. I'd always cut the fuses extry long so we had plenty of time to set the shot and get out. Sometimes we'd go back too quick, and if you breathed of that smoke, you'd get the dynamite headache. It'd just about blind you with pain. Winter was always itching to get started, and then he'd come stumbling out, holding his big wooly head, and he'd moan for hours. I'd say Winter, you got your still up in there? And he'd moan. It wasn't no fun, that headache, but it never killed a man.

When we started that tunnel, we begin on each side of the mountain, and somehow we were able to meet exact in the middle. If that warn't pure luck, I don't know what is. As soon as we shovelled out all the rock and muled it away, we run in the track. The tunnel was just big enough for the standard gauge engine to squeak through. We all threw our hats in the air when it come poking out the other side. We'd done it.

Then the logging companies had full sway over the hills. I never seen so much work and so many jobs. They was begging for help. My wages went to almost three dollars a day to build the railroad grades, cut ties, lay them rails, and run switchbacks up the ridges. We put roads all through that country. When I logged, Winter and I'd each take the end of a crosscut saw, and he could jerk me off my feet. He could beat me sawing any day, so I liked working the trains better, and mostly stayed a brakeman on the engines and serviced the roads.

As word got around about the works, people moved into the hollers all through Red River. Tar paper shacks spread from

Nada, past the tunnel and down the other side. And all through that country, everything started changing.

Except my luck. Once our train was hauling logs from around Indian Creek. We switchbacked up the ridge and stopped, and I jumped off the log car. The next feller that jumped was Jim Strunk, but the engine grabbed and he slipped. Them big wheels slid right across him and cut off his legs. Somebody rode for the saddle-pocket doc at Furnace Mountain, but he could't do much. He pulled some whiskey from his pouches and staved back the blood as best he could. The company rushed Jim by special train to the Lexington hospital, and he didn't die for a long time. Anyways, I was living up to my nickname. But nobody knew, not even me, that the best of my luck was yet to come.

It was a real sight, those years, to see the land open up. All the roads we built and the log trains hauling over them, the teams of oxen and giant horses, hillside after hillside falling down. Oh, it's really something to see what men can do when they set their minds to it. Everybody was making good that wanted to. Ever little holler had shanties in them, and things got more social. Most fellers liked a good time, and parties and square dances started up almost every weekend.

I thought a dance was the best fun of all. I could do everything—call, play the fiddle, and dance too. Different people'd have the dances at their homes, but most usually we'd set up places in the woods—go back the track a ways and make a platform. Then spread the word. Come evening the people'd be flocking in. We'd sweep around the platform floor, sprinkle it with corn meal so dancers wouldn't slip, the banjos, fiddles and guitars would tune up, and away we'd go.

Winter and me took turns calling because we both wanted to dance. Every weekend more girls would come and ever time a new face showed up, all the bachelors would rush in for a try-out. Me, I just liked having a good time. By then I was twenty-two, making good, and couldn't see getting serious about much. But I'd say to Winter, When is an old man like you going to get down to business? And he'd laugh and say,

Why are you trying to hurry me to my grave, and me just an innocent boy? But I could tell different. He'd eye every new girl, but he never seemed to get anywheres with them, at least not with the ones you'd want. But he tried. Lord, did he try. Why is it sometimes that them who risk the most never get what they want? Luck is the only answer I know.

One night the sky had gone gunpowder dark and the lanterns were jiggling with the music. It was a big dance. Had three or four fiddlers and a couple of banjos and I don't know how many people dancing around me. Winter was calling out "Leather Britches," stomping his foot, that big old head just wagging. Suddenly he stopped, then picked up again in a beat, but everybody turned to see what he was gawking at. Three new girls had strolled up from the river. Couldn't see brother or daddy with them but all three looked good, and one was about the prettiest thing I ever saw. She couldn't have been more than thirteen or fourteen, but she had thick corn-tassle hair, and eyes big and brown as sassafras in your cup. They stood in a bunch, and one by one the fellers not already dancing started swarming in close. As soon as the song ended, I got rid of Jenny and went to stand my turn in line, but the little one wouldn't dance with anybody. Her sisters went every set, but she just sat there. I asked her once, and she said no. So I forgot about her and enjoyed myself. Winter tried and tried, but she put him off like everybody else.

All the next week he mooned around. He was doing extry crew work with me, unloading ballast and jacking up the track. I told him, You better watch out what you're doing, or that tamping hammer's going to hit the wrong thing. He already looked like somebody's hit him over the head. All he'd talk about was Mary Potter this, Mary Potter that, if he said anything, period. And I'd remark, You got the dynamite headache without the bang. And he'd laugh, but then that sick look would spread back over his face again.

Next weekend come the dance and Winter was no account at all. He wouldn't pick the guitar and couldn't be propped up there to call more than one song at a time. The three sisters was there again, just the same as before. I got to hand it to

Winter for trying, but she wouldn't have a thing to do with him or anybody.

I got tired of calling. After "Idy Red," I quit and turned it over to Noah Jones. I stepped back in the woods for a sip or two, then come back and watched the dancing. I couldn't help myself—I looked Mary over again. She sat on the side of the platform, thin and light, her blonde hair kind of flowing over her shoulders and down her back like the sun pouring over water. She looked so sweet, she could have been taffy wrapped in a blue calico dress. I couldn't help it—my mouth went dry when I saw she was watching me—a glance here and a glance there, almost like the flickering of the lanterns. But then I knew. I decided to give her one more chance. I circled around the platform, walked up and stood right before her. I asked her the best I could. I said, Please, Miss Mary, would you share the next set with me?

Her cheeks flushed, and she didn't look at me direct, but she said, All right, Mr. White.

She knew my name—I'd guessed right. So we danced, and I didn't try nothing fancy. I could see the fellers' heads jerking in our direction, and I knew I had the laugh. Winter was standing off to the side, fists shoved in his pockets, staring at us too. He'd disappear into the trees and then come back and stare. Well, once she started dancing, that little girl wouldn't stop. She skipped me from one set to another. Before I knew it, the fiddles were slowing and the lanterns bobbing off toward the river. I handed her back to her sisters and didn't even ask to walk her home or nothing. I just thanked her, and she smiled sweet and little and low. She might have been awful young, but she knew more than you'd guess. When she turned, I waved, then headed down the tracks toward Eddards Branch where I was shantying.

I didn't see Winter anywhere, and I didn't see him the whole next week. Somebody said he'd gone logging over in the Big Woods on Tarr Ridge. But it was a fast week, really. A Shay engine broke down by Switchback Holler and I was servicing it. By then, I knew every bolt of those trains and could fix anything. There warn't too many in that country who knew what I did.

I didn't see him at the next dance either. I started the calling. Now that takes somebody special—without a good caller, a dance won't get in tune or step. The caller calls the shots, and if he knows what he's doing, they can come hot and fast. Mary was there again, but not many fooled with her—they could see which way the land was lying. Besides, one or two new faces had joined the crowd. I looked them over, but wasn't too interested. Mary was watching me all the time and smiling her little, sugar smile.

Then I saw Winter. He had on a shirt so white it glared and he'd tried to plaster his hair back with something, but it kept popping out of place. He'd run a big raw hand over it, but it didn't do no good. He was wearing boots so new he looked like he was tippy-toeing when he walked, and worst of all, he was stuffed into his dress-up britches. I'd only seen them once before, at his ma's funeral when he was two years thinner. He oozed through the crowd to Mary, and I know what he asked and I know what she said. It was a pitiful sight, a big man making a fool of himself over a little girl. He tried four dances in a row, but her face clammed up and turned dark. The last dance I called, he was begging again. Somebody laughed. He tried to shove them fists into his pockets but his pants were too tight. Then he shoved into the trees instead. But he stayed around. I know he was out there, watching and hitting the bottle. I know him. I went and shouted to him, but he wouldn't answer. What the hell, I said, That ain't no way to be.

I went back and Mary was sitting there, smiling at me. A sister to her was smiling at me too, but I didn't pay her no mind. I asked Mary to dance and she said all right. And when the dance broke up, I asked to walk her home, and she said all right again. So me and Mary and the sisters laughed and had a good time all the way to Dunkans Branch. I thanked them at the door but didn't go in. I didn't want to press my luck. I didn't even press Mary's hand.

I strolled toward the railroad grade and turned to go home, and up the track I saw someone standing in the moonlight. I guess I knew he'd be waiting. I walked up and said, Hold on, Winter. Let's talk this out. But I couldn't believe it. He looked dead calm, like a snake charming a bird. I stepped closer.

I've got no say over that girl's mind. I can't help it if she's chose me over you, I said.

His lips trembled—he must have been drunk. I couldn't stand it any longer. I said, Why don't you act like a man for once! Then I reached back and hit him as hard as I could. He just seemed surprised, but his arm flew out in defense and caught me in the face as I leaned into him. I crashed back against the rails. It all felt the way a train must feel running into you. I thought, now he's going to crush me—those shiny boots were right next to my head. But he didn't. He just stood there a while, his face looking sadder and sadder. Then he stooped and lightly ran his hand over my hair. Finally he said, I wouldn't never hurt you, Elmer, never do you the way you've done me. You've traded on that too long. Just don't ever fool yourself into thinking you know what you are, and that it's something plain and honest. You and me will always know different.

I didn't even hear him leave. I just shut my eyes and lay there awhile, didn't feel much of anything. Then I tried to move. I put my hand to my face and it come back wet and dark. Where my nose was supposed to be was a pounding like a tamping hammer. I tried to get mad, but I wasn't, really. Instead, I was getting happy. Things was settled between him and me once and for all. And I'd beaten him.

My nose was broke and I lost two teeth, but it was worth it. I have to say I warn't as good looking as before, but Mary took me anyway. I married a child, but I've never had regrets. She's as fine a thing as I ever would have got.

I built a log house not far from Furnace Mountain and we settled down. We've been married two years and I kindly hope my boy's eyes will stay blue like his daddy's. I like to hold him and think of the good times we're going to have. I'll teach him how to hunt and fish, I'll show him where to find sing, and I'll point out all the works his daddy's done. I helped change this country from pure wilderness to what it is today. It'll be wonderful for him to see them big grades and roads and the tunnel and know I accomplished that. Making something out of nothing—you're lucky if you can do it.

Planting Time

Aurell Pearson: Laurel Creek, 1924

The first time I saw Laura Hern, I was a fourteen-year-old boy. It's a day that sticks with me, but not because of her. Not at first, anyway.

I start remembering with me and Martha planting pumpkins. Dad took off to Furnace Mountain for supplies and left us to work. Where he got so much pumpkin seeds and how he thought we'd eat it, if it all come up, I've never figured out. We would've choked it down ever meal—fried, stewed, dried, canned, pied—and given away to everybody on Red River, and still had plenty left. So it didn't make sense to me or Martha, either one. But you didn't argue with Dad. He said a thing and if you remarked different, it was like pulling back the trigger on a rifle.

It was a terrible hot day, I remember that too. Martha and me poked in the ground till we felt like woodpeckers, drilling holes and dropping in a fistful of seeds. But still the bucket was half full, and we were stuck down at what I call the Pumpkin Bottom. Boy, it was hot. My face was trickling and my back was itching. And the river was right close by. Where Laurel Creek fell into the river, the soil gathered rich and black. Daddy knew just where to plant the easiest and the best, as close to the creek as we could get. Well, the creek run deep and clear as a bell at its mouth, and I could see schools of white suckers in there, and red-eyes and chubb—oh, it was crowded.

It just so happened we had our poles baited and stuck in the bank up a ways. I said, Martha, I do believe they's as many fish in that creek today as pumpkin seeds in here.

I looked down in the bucket and sighed. Then I said, Let's throw the rest in the river.

Martha thought about it for a spell. She was always smart, Martha was. Even then she didn't have no looks, but she was smart enough to keep out of people's way. Not like me. She fingered them seeds light and dry in her hands and said, These seeds will float. If they get caught in Daddy's trot lines, he'll know for sure.

I looked at Martha and knew right then that she'd get by in this world. So we dug a hole so deep I knew nothing could straggle out. Then I dumped in the seeds, and they poured out like a string of blind little eyes. We covered them real good and stomped down hard.

I patted my wet shirt against my chest. Let's go cool off in the river first.

You go on, Martha said. She had kind of milky blue eyes, like a marble, and one wasn't quite straight, so she never seemed to be looking at you even if she was. When she started to cry, like now, she made a real sight, I can tell you.

Oh, cat's got your tongue, huh, I said and laughed. She just wiped her face, took the bucket and headed for the creek. So I went to the river by myself and was glad of it. See, our swimming hole was too close to where Dad had done the shooting. In the spring, kittens were crawling all over the barn and house, and when Uncle Rudy come for a visit, he and Dad had a round-up. Cats, kittens, all they could get hold of, they stuffed into a burlap bag and went laughing toward the river. By the time we got down to the bank, they'd just dumped it in the water and started target practice. The sack jerked, made little noises and sank, and Martha started screaming. Dad was awful mad we'd followed and ruined their sport. He started yelling, while Uncle Rudy stood to the side with his arms folded over his belly, his eyebrows raised and bristling like hog hair. Martha and I took off and kept in the woods till almost dark. By then, both of them was heavy asleep, and it passed over.

So now I had the run of the river. I threw my clothes on a stump, slid down the bank and jumped in. The river'd risen and then fell after a big rain, and the water was green and cool and quiet. I just paddled around for a while, ducking my head under and trying to miss the logs sunk by the far side. Then I pulled back up the bank, grabbed my stuff and walked to the creek where Martha was. I rebaited my pole and settled against the sycamore. Its bark curled rough against my back, and I could scratch all I wanted.

I've always loved fishing, and Martha was a good hand at it too, especially making coffee-sack seines. On up the creek we made a mud dam to catch hog suckers. We set our lard can in the center of it, and kind of flattened it so it was wide. Then we muddied the water even more—we figured that way the fish couldn't see too good. I'd get Martha to run up the creek and scare the fish. It didn't take her long. They'd hit that can— bang! bang! bang! And I'd jerk it up!

I'm sorry. I could talk fish all day, and I guess it don't matter. And it don't matter that a couple of weeks later Dad checked the field and found a huge clump of pumpkins all coming up together. And maybe it don't even matter how things broke between him and me.

Well, we hadn't been sitting on the bank too long when we heard a wagon creaking up the river path. A sorrel nag I didn't know plodded into view, lathering in his harness. By the set of his head he looked like he'd come some distance, and two strangers sat in the wagon. The man had his hands full, talking to himself and sawing at the reins, trying to keep the wheels between the mud ruts and the rocks. He looked wore out, too. The most I remember about the girl was that she looked big and strange—and stiff. Yeah, like a heap of barn lumber, stiff on that seat. They turned up our holler.

I guess it was a good day after all, at least for the fish, because Martha and me pulled in our lines, hid our poles, and went after the wagon. It didn't stop at our place, but swayed up the hill to old man Hern's. That's all we knew for a while, except that an hour later the man and wagon come back down and left toward Furnace Mountain.

Now, I'm not sure if you'd call Isaiah Hern a neighbor or

not. He did live up there—had a good cleared space and a big, four-room house all to himself. But he never came down, and he never spoke to us. I always saw him at a distance. He wore a long white beard and black suits. And a black cap with a bill on it. Yes, he stayed dressed like a gentleman—I'm sure that's what he thought he was. He grew roses in his yard, and we always figured he had a lot of money, if not friendliness. He had kin, both in Furnace Mountain and in Campton, and from time to time they'd bring stores for him, but they never stayed long.

She did stay, I guess to wait on him. When Ma went down to church a few weeks later, she heard the girl was related some ways, and had come from Lexington. All we could do was guess if she was orphaned or what—them Herns was always a close-mouthed bunch. I didn't pay her much mind. I didn't have time. We was kept busy in the fields—the bottom corn was doing real good and Dad aimed for us to keep it that way. In July he had a chance to railroad up around the Koomer Dip, and he was thirsty for some cash money, if you know what I mean. So he left, and with the hoeing and the chopping and the hunting, I kept busy.

That's how things went for a while till Dad come back. We'd got our crops laid by when one evening he pushed away from the supper table and said from out of nowhere, School's started for the year. You younguns better get to it, or it'll be done over.

Momma was nodding along with him, like she always did. I could feel my dinner churning inside me. Dad's face had the same mule smile it always had when he studied me over, which wasn't too often. At times he wasn't a bad looking man. His cheeks were chiseled and shaved, his eyes sharp, his hair dark as charred wood. Some people might have called him little, but not to his face, because he had a body as tough as barbed wire and he was a man of no excuses. I was glad I didn't look a thing like him.

You don't care nothing about school, I said, my face feeling hot. He just smiled more.

You go tomorrow, he said, leaning his chair against the

wall. He propped his head back, his eyes lazy and half-closed, but he was watching and waiting.

I didn't say nothing more, but just walked out. It would be dark soon. The light was still hitting the big stone lip of the cliff across the river, but it was all shadow here in the holler, and lapping cool. Up the creek, the laurel grew in traps and snares. A body could get lost in it easy—only I knew the woods too well. I wandered along the bank, to where the water poured like lead into the river. The mist was flowing in and bats were zigzagging low between the trees. Mosquitoes began whining around my ears. Here and there I heard a ripple, the flip of a fish, and a wing came close by me. Then I heard Momma calling, her voice raspy and raw as usual. Snakes would be moving with the night and the damp. I stood a few minutes more, the mosquitoes feeling almost good. But I had to go back. The moon hadn't topped the ridges yet, and I followed the black squirm of the creek across the bottom toward home. I saw Momma had lit the lamp.

It was at school the next day I saw Laura Hern up close for the first time. The kids was already in groups working when Martha and me got there. Miss Frieman wasn't too happy to see us, I could tell. She looked up from her desk, frowned, then smiled a little. Then she stood, straightened her blouse and said, Hello Martha, hello Aurell. If you're going to come to school, then be on time. You're behind everyone else already.

I didn't care what she thought. For me, the best part of school was the two mile walk. She handed me a tablet left over from last year and a pencil, and told me to get to work. My books were still in the desk where I'd left them. I guessed I was in the fourth grade again, for the third time. We couldn't afford a new set of books, so I just had to use these. Now, Laura Hern sat against the wall and by herself. When Miss Frieman asked her a question, she talked different than us, snippy if you ask me. She had sixth grade books she knew all the answers from. She'd open one, her face round like a turnip, and get close to the page. Her lips would move, and she'd fiddle with her fat braids. In five minutes she'd be done and then just stare out the window. She didn't say nothing to us, only a word or so to the Hern boys from Furnace Mountain, and they mostly left her alone. When Martha and me walked home in the afternoon, she dallied behind us. She passed our house without a word. I stood in the door and watched her, them socks and shoes mincing through the mud, that flowered dress swinging, clover-colored.

By the third day of school I'd had it. I'd done read my books through twice, and what I didn't know two years before I still couldn't figure out. And Miss Frieman was getting switch-happy, prodding me over my sums. Seems like she was always standing behind me, crowding my back. When it come time for water from the cold-spring, I couldn't wait, though I was surprised Miss Frieman let me go with Frank Hern. The bucket felt good, its handle rolling through my hand, and by the spring the mud oozed cool through my toes. Now Frank had always seemed to like a joke as good as I did. I filled the bucket almost full, but when I unbuttoned my fly and let go, he wouldn't follow suit. He laughed and egged me on, but that was all.

Miss Frieman was in a worse mood when we got back, wondering why we'd taken so long. She was hot like the rest of us, unbuttoning and buttoning her collar and pinning back her stray hair. All the kids gathered around the bucket with their tin cans, and I winked at Frank. He was standing back with his two brothers. The little ones got theirs and I saw Laura Hern take a gulp. I tried not to grin. I even let Martha fill her can.

The trouble began with Miss Frieman. She smelled her glass and said, Boys, where did you get this water?

Smooth as cat fur, Frank said, Aurell made it.

Her sweaty face turned white underneath and hard as the peeled switch lying on her desk. She whacked Frank some, but she took a vengeance on me. Frank and his brothers thought it was a real scream. They didn't dare laugh, but I could see it in their eyes. After school they took off fast for Furnace Mountain. I felt like I'd sat on blackberry brambles all day. I wanted to hit something. Even Martha hung back when we walked home. What's Daddy going to do if he hears, she just kept mumbling.

I turned on her. If you don't try Frank Hern's trick he may not find out, leastways not for a while.

When I yelled, Martha threw up a hand to protect her face, but I didn't hit her. I just yanked her frizzy black hair. No, I saw Laura Hern behind us, and I waited for her. She almost run into me before she slowed down. I said, How come you never talk to us?

Her gray eyes looked over my head. She was tall enough to do it. She tried to edge past.

You ain't fit under our feet. Pearsons don't yellow-tale, like Herns, I said and stepped closer.

You get out of my way, she said, drawing herself up. You're the dirt—everybody says so.

She looked as prudish and stocky a thing as I've ever seen in a skirt. I clamped onto both of her arms and almost had to climb up her, but I kissed her, hard. Before I could bite her lip, she shoved me against a ledge by the road and knocked me down. When she spit at me, I laughed and said, Yellow-tale and ugly too.

I grabbed for her ankles, but all I got was a handful of sock. Her face was swelling up even bigger than it usually was, and she jumped loose and ran down the path. I thought she was crying, but it was just Martha, giggling.

Shut up, I told her, and her mouth sealed tight. She got the lunch pail Laura had dropped, but I jerked it away and threw it toward the river. I would have filled it with something for her if I could have sat down long enough to do it.

I got to school even later the next day, and I had Martha go in first. Miss Frieman stood, touched her collar, and told the class to go out and play where the weeds was cut and low. She had me and all the Herns stay behind. She looked as stern as I had ever seen her, the two creases getting real deep between her eyes.

Aurell, Laura told me you kissed her against her will after school yesterday. Is this true?

Yellow-tale, I said.

Miss Frieman slapped me. That'll do, she said. I won't stand for this kind of behavior. It's disgusting. I don't know what you do at home, but you're not going to bully around here. Now you apologize.

I wouldn't. She had me lean against the cold iron of the stove and then she wore me out. She was a stronger woman than she looked. But what I hated most was her having them Herns watch the whole thing. Frank looked smug and was nudging his brothers. And Laura looked most satisfied, her face the color of boiled meal. She was smiling at me at last. Miss Frieman asked her if she wanted a turn with the switch, but of course she wouldn't have nothing to do with it.

And then, later, there was Dad. I was dragging a log from the woods when I saw Miss Frieman ride up our road. I watched from behind a tree. Dad was lying around on the front porch, and he didn't even stand when she stopped at the steps and got down. I couldn't hear what they said, and she didn't stay long, but I swear I heard Dad laughing. That's when she pulled herself back up on her paint horse and trotted away.

I couldn't quite figure it, and kept hid for a while. When he looked asleep again, I tried to sneak past to the back door. Without moving, he said, You, boy, come here.

He opened his eyes, stretched big, and scratched under his arm. He didn't undo his belt like I thought he would, but he had me follow him behind the barn to where the laurel thickets started. I could feel Momma watching us. When he turned, he was smiling too, like the others had done. But he said, I guess you're a big boy now. And he put out his hand as if to shake mine. I started to nod and then he said, Well, let's see.

He hit me across the face. I threw out my arm and clipped him on the neck. Then he slammed into me and I fell. I twisted against the laurel roots, but before I could get up, he kicked me, and then he kicked me again. I begin to lose track of my back and legs, and a sound like a saw buzzed through my ears. Something hit my head and everything fuzzed white.

I couldn't have been out for long. All I could see was the

laurel dark above me. When I tried to sit up, my back wrenched on fire. All I could do was lie there—maybe I passed out again. I don't know. Finally I was able to get to the house. Dad was sitting on the porch, with his eyes closed. I dragged to bed, and Ma brought water and washed me off, but didn't say nothing, not even about me crying. Neither did Martha, when she brought me dinner. I tried to eat a little, but threw it back up. Still, I hid some bread under the pillow for later. I couldn't get out of bed for two days. Then come Monday morning, Dad lounged in by the bed and said, Get out of there and get to school.

It took me an hour longer to walk there, but I made it. Martha helped me. I never spoke again to any of them Herns, and they stayed clear of me. And it wasn't long till Dad had me help house the tobacco we was tending down by Gladie. I didn't have no more time for school that year.

And things changes. The world comes your way, or at least leaves you alone. By school time the next year, I'd shot up three inches. I'd thinned corn for Otis Brown and he'd slapped me on the shoulder, pronounced me a good hand, and give me fifty cents a day. I earned it, and it looked big as a wagon wheel. I bought me some gallus overalls and a blue shirt, and wore them to school when I got around to going. We had a new teacher, Miss Woods, and she wasn't much older than me. The first time she poked me with her switch, I broke it into little pieces. And she never said a word. I ain't sorry I never finished the fourth grade. Not usually, anyway. I've got by and it hasn't been on books.

And if I didn't go to school much that summer, neither did Laura Hern.

Buddy, I must have had the kiss of death, even then. During that first winter after she come, she got down right poor. I saw her the day they took her out. They had to pass our house. The snow was melting fast and the ice hissing apart on the river, still a wagon couldn't get through. They had to carry her. Her face was shrank in and her lips as white as the river fog. She had the consumption, we heard, and old Isaiah couldn't tend to her. So he was left alone again with his clerical shirts and his summer roses, and they took her to the Herns in Furnace Mountain. Old Isaiah was lucky. He lived a right smart longer.

She died. And one by one all them Herns took it and died too, even Frank. Or so I heard from time to time. I was long gone before then. See, I got me a public job at a saw mill off Dunwoldy Creek, wheeling sawdust and carrying water for the workmen. It was a eight mile walk—four miles each way. But it was worth the seventy-five cents a day, and I kept it all myself, except what I let Ma and Martha wheedle out of me. Dad was supposed to be over at the Koomer Dip, cutting ties, but who knows where he was. I never saw him again. When the mill closed down that fall, I left the river, and didn't come back for twenty-three years.

There Is a River

Maggie Hern: Gladie Creek, 1926

We say we work hard all our lives, but we don't. So much of the time people are too little or too old, or sick. It's then I see them, mostly at the beginning and at the end. I know what I shouldn't know. I ain't a gossip, though—I keep their miseries to myself, and I comfort as I can. But I don't have patience no more with people sorry for theirselves because they're old—so few gets the chance. How many have I brought into this world for too short a time, or for so little purpose.

I thought that when I looked at Elmer and his little boy, and I saw we'd have to get them in the ground quick. They'd gone too long already. Mary was sitting in the rocker, her face empty but for the light coming through the window. Her chair creaked and sighed through the heat of the room. I touched her shoulder.

Mary, honey, I said, I think it best all the way around if we bury them as soon as George makes the coffins.

She just stared out the window. George nudged me. He'd brought the saw horses from the barn. We arranged them in pairs and set planks on top. When he helped me lift the bodies across them, his face screwed shut against the smell, then he hurried out to cobble up them coffins as fast as he could.

I straightened the clothes on the bodies and put nickels on their eyes. I was glad Mary was sitting by the window. I could hardly stand to touch the face of her little boy, and to see

Elmer like this . . . somehow, laying out the dead never gets easier. I thought it would, but it don't. I covered them both over with sheets.

I walked back to Mary and tried again. I said what I know Elmer would have—I've done what I can. It'd be a kindness to everybody to bury them before dark.

She looked at me and smiled. No, she said, it ain't right. Not till morning. You know they was just found.

Her smile spread terrible big, then her face snapped together, all empty. She had a sock of Elmer's in her lap, and her fingers were squirming in and out of its holes. She got her sewing basket and started mending it, her eyes dry and harsh as cinders.

I don't ever force nobody. I left her alone. I rinsed some cloths in cool water and put them on the faces, then I sat down. The only sounds was the rock of Mary's chair, the clatter of George out back, and the drone of bees under the porch eaves. The sun was bending over the hills. Soon as milking time got past, folks would be coming to set out the night. The room was stuffy, filled with the green-black crawling stink of the bodies, worse than a heap of rotten potatoes or something a dog would roll in.

I looked at Mary, her hands still in her lap. Her cheeks was almost clear in the sun, and her hair nested back in a bun, neat and honey colored. I've always thought her as sweet-turned a girl as I ever waited on. I had helped with both her babies and did the best I could, though only the one boy made it through. Even with the last and the worst I was there. If Elmer hadn't been a third cousin—well, I'd have gone, but who would have wanted to? The beginning of December and storming wild. I'm used to the knock on the night door, but that time the rain was so hard, I thought it was the storm pounding. When Luke got up, though, it was Elmer. I'll never forget him standing there, little Elmer hugging his legs, the black wall of rain behind them.

He said, Please, please hurry, Maggie. Mary is took sick real bad.

Luke said, Get in here and warm up, Elmer. He slammed

the door behind them. Then he said, Now what's going on?

Elmer rubbed the water from his eyes and said, I thought it best to bring Elmer when I come, if you don't mind tending to him. He won't be no trouble, he said, looking hard at little Elmer.

Luke glanced at me and back at them. He said, Fine, that's fine.

I smiled at the boy and took his hat. My own kids were rustling around in the loft. George, I called out, you all keep quiet up there. It's just Elmer White.

Maggie please, Elmer said, get ready. We got to go.

Luke sighed, got his lantern and said, I'll go saddle the mule.

No, Elmer said, talking faster, I already got Sam Green's horse—borrowed her for the mill tomorrow. Sure didn't know I'd need her tonight. He looked at me again.

I didn't say another word. I got dressed in the back room and put on my coat, and checked the pockets for things I might need.

Luke was saying, I thought Mary's time wasn't till around February.

Well, you know she's had trouble before, Elmer said and hustled me toward the door.

Luke opened it. I don't like this at all, he said. I better ride along, at least a ways. I'll go saddle Sally.

But Elmer pushed past and almost shouted, Don't fret so much, Luke! There ain't time to wait. He tugged me outside and yanked the reins loose from the fence. The poor horse was still heaving and steaming in the rain. He mounted and give me a hand, his fingers icy and slick. Luke was grumbling beside me and pushing my legs up and over. Then I was behind the saddle and grabbing onto Elmer. He wheeled the horse, and Luke and the house were left behind. Elmer pushed the horse along as fast as we dared to go. It was only a mile from Furnace Mountain to their place by Gladie Creek, but it's hard to say how long it took us to get there. The rain had dug past my coat and was sleet in my face, when the horse worked her way over a ledge and down a ridgeside.

I yelled in Elmer's ear, Thank God we don't have to cross the river. I couldn't hear what he said back, and the mare was splashing up to her knees before I begin worrying about the creek. Suddenly she shied sideways and almost fell. Elmer started kicking at her furious. She straightened and lunged forward. Water poured into my boots.

I screamed, Lord have mercy, Elmer, turn back! The creek's from hill to hill.

Then water come up on my knees, even with the mare as big as she was, and strong. The water rushed at us, black and hard. Something hit me, lashing and tangled, and I threw my arm out. The branches went on. I felt the horse lift off, drift sideways. I screamed and hid my face against Elmer's back. Water covered my chin, mud and foam choking. We was going under. We'd have to get off the horse. Then the mare's hooves come solid under her, and she staggered against the current. With a snort she lurched higher, and we were clear.

Elmer jumped off and slid me down. I was scared almost out of my head. He held me close for a moment and said, It's all right now. You done real fine. Then he laughed, scared a little himself—When we come through here before, it wasn't past the mare's legs.

I was shaking and so was the horse, so bad we had to walk the last little way. When I fell down, Elmer pulled me up, my clothes were that heavy with water. I slipped again and hit a tree. No, it was a porch pillar—I hadn't even seen the lighted window. Elmer snatched the door open, then slammed it behind us. Suddenly it was quiet, away from the storm.

A flame, low and mean and without heat, flared in the fireplace. I looked for Mary, and saw her in the bed by the wall. I went to her and for a moment thought she was dead. Her eyes seemed locked open and I couldn't see her breathing.

Mary, I said and touched her cheek. It was warmer than my hand. I leaned closer and she blinked, her eyes focusing on me.

Maggie, she whispered.

I laughed, relieved, and said, Honey, what on top of the earth! Just couldn't you have put this off!

The corners of her mouth moved again, as if she was trying

to smile, and water come down her face. I was dripping all over her.

I'm sorry, honey, I said, standing back, I'm getting you wet. I tried to get my coat off, but it stuck to my arms. So I pulled the quilts from around her instead. They was sticky and brown, blood seeping all through them. I tucked them back around her and said, There, that's better. It won't be long now. I'm going to wait on you good. You know I will.

I kept smiling and glanced at Elmer. His face was froze like he'd seen a nest of spiders under the covers. He turned and went in the other room. You rest now, I told Mary, squeezing her hand.

Then Elmer come back with some dry clothes of his—I'd never have fit into Mary's. It warn't no time for embarrassment. He helped me with my coat, then I took the britches, shirt and sweater and thanked him. You was right to hurry us, Elmer, I said. He nodded and busied himself in the kitchen so I could get dressed. He'd said he'd banked up the stove before he left, so now it was easy to fire it. That night he worked hard. He filled the kettle and some pots and set them to heat. He built up the fire in the grate and brought me sheets to tear for bandages. Then he hurried outside to the horse.

Mary lay so awful weak and unnatural quiet. When the room glowed and smoked warmer, I lifted back the quilts again and wiped some of the blood off her. Elmer shivered back inside and threw off his coat. He started ripping up bandages and shoving them toward me.

Law's sake, Elmer, I said, get into dry clothes yourself or I'll have you to care for, too.

I didn't mean to snap, but he hadn't even taken time to warm his hands or dry his face, and his twisty nose was dripping all the way down to his chin. Oh, I shouldn't have been so short with him, but I was. I turned back to Mary. Before I knew it, he'd changed, washed, and was carrying hot water from the stove. And he assisted me. For the other baby, he'd hung around and was kindly in the way—never was I asked so many questions, and I didn't like him poking around. It wasn't quite right, was different from the other men I knew. Now I was glad. I guess we hadn't been there more than an hour when the baby come, and Mary couldn't help hardly. It took the two of us to pull that baby into this world. And Lord, I could see it wasn't going to stay long—just a pitiful mite of flesh, and not breathing good. And it was smiling. I cut the cord, dried it all over, and rubbed hard on its chest and back, but nothing seemed to help much.

Finally Elmer said, Aw, let me hold him. He cuddled him into one of his shirts for luck, then wrapped a blanket around him. He showed Mary and said, Oh, Mother, he's beautiful. But when he tried to put him in her arms, she just passed out. The blood was flowing worse.

The rest of the night I kept packing bandages around her, trying to hold back the blood, and her sinking deeper under the quilts. I even tried packing with spider webs, and hid a handful of feathers under the bed. Elmer rocked before the fire, snuggling that baby close, maybe dozing but never loosening his grip. That's a scene I won't never forget. The man in the chair, getting up only to throw more wood on the fire, shoring it with coal, the rain sizzling on the flames, the outside roar of wind, the stillness of the woman, and the silence of blood. Finally, the lamp sputtered out. It was morning, thin and gray. And with the creeping of the light, her bleeding slowed, stopped and shrank back, as if afraid, deciding to stay in the body and not desert it. I don't know what turned it around. It warn't me. That is the only certain thing.

I was easing away some clotted rags when I felt Elmer standing beside me. He still held the baby, its blanket smudged with coal. I turned, and his eyes were dark blue and smeared like his fire-dirty hands. I answered the question he didn't ask. Yes, I said, the blood's stopped. If it don't start again, and she has enough left, I think she may pull through.

He didn't even smile, though a change come over his face. I can't say exactly what—I guess I didn't look too close. I walked to the fire and threw the rags on it, and the smell of scorched blood smoked up heavy. I saw Elmer put the baby next to Mary, lay it down as gentle as any woman.

I'd take a caution, I said. She's not awake yet. She might roll on it. Here, I'll hold him for a spell.

But Elmer dragged my chair from the bed and brought it by

his at the fireplace. No, he said, she'll not hurt him. He touched my shoulder and motioned me to sit. He sat too. He said, You must be wore out. Why don't you rest for a minute? I'm going to make us some coffee—I think we both need it.

It did feel good in the rocker. He was right. I hadn't known how tired I was. I raised my pant cuffs, and there was big lumps and bruises where I'd fallen and where Elmer'd kicked me instead of the horse. The warmth of the fire climbed my legs and arms, and I leaned back and closed my eyes. Then I woke up. I heard a choking sound, and hurried to the bed. Inside its cover, the baby lay cold and still—it'd been dead for a while. Mary hadn't changed. I heard the sound again, coming from the kitchen. I stood in the door. The kettle was boiling on the stove and the coffee pot was letting rich thick steam into the air. Elmer was sitting beside two mugs he'd put on the table. His hands covered his face, and the sound come again. I didn't know what to do. The tears come in my own eyes, and my chest hurt.

I walked to the table and said, Elmer, for heaven's sake, get a hold of yourself! Something accusing twisted my words, and I was ashamed. But my anger come out stronger. I never seen anything like this, I said and rapped the table. You got to hold onto yourself—we ain't all gone to our final home yet. You got to think of the living.

He stopped shaking, but kept his eyes hid in his hands. I filled his cup. Here, drink this, I said. It'll buck you up. He wiped his face with his fingers and took hold of the coffee. He just stared at it.

I poured some in my own mug. I said, the Lord gives and He takes away. You've seen His marvels, Elmer, and know His mysterious ways. You have to trust in Him, and He'll give you strength.

Elmer kept his eyes lowered, and the coffee burned hot and bitter on my tongue. You want some sugar? I said.

He said no.

I got some for myself. There didn't seem much else to say. Elmer wouldn't look at me. He knew I'd seen something in him that was shameful for a man. But I've seen the shame of many people, one way or another, and it's why they call me again, though they don't like me for what I see. But that they don't never say—we don't never say what we should.

Elmer took a sip, like he was being polite, then stood. I got to check the stock, he said flatly. He picked up his muddy boots by the door and hauled them on. His coat hadn't dried, but he put it on anyway. Rain peppered in as he left. I kept drinking my coffee, and prayed in my head for him and his little baby, and for us all. I poured myself another cup and before it was gone, Elmer had returned, snowflakes glistening on his shoulders, his pockets bulging. Now that he was working again, he seemed brighter. He took out five eggs and said, We're lucky, This snow may slow the water down. I'm afraid it's a bad tide in the river, Mag. He took off his coat and swallowed the cold coffee in his cup. The horse, he said, she's doing better too. I thought she might be down this morning, but she's all right. He said these fast, like a kind of defense. I just let him alone. Besides, it was my turn outside.

I stepped onto the porch, and it looked like all the water in the world had gone crazy. The creek and river had jumped their banks and rammed together. They was spreading everywhere. The air was mired with sleet and the start of ice. What was left of the ground was gray with mud and the cling of new snow. If this kept up, pretty soon the privy would be underwater. I hurried in. When I come out, a shouting echoed from across the creek. I yelled and walked closer. The snow swirled around and I saw the outline of a man on a mule.

Maggie, is that you? he called out. It was Luke.

I yelled back. He had a bundle under one of his arms, but he must have thought the creek too wide even to throw it across.

It's flooding terrible ever where, he shouted. We're all right. Are you? How's Mary?

I yelled again, but I don't know if he heard me. The wind was blowing hard my way and the snow thickened. I lost sight of him. When I finally saw him again, he shouted and waved. Then Sally turned back up the ridge. Good old Luke. He'd come to help as he could, but the water in the middle rushed fast and deep, and bristled with logs. How we'd ever made it across in the dark the night before I'll never know.

My coat and hat was still clammy, the wind freezing through them. Now I couldn't even see much of the water for the snow. I hurried back inside the house. Elmer had biscuits baking in the oven and was getting ready to fry some eggs. I shook off my coat and checked on Mary. She still hadn't got awake. The baby and its wrappings were gone. Neither Elmer or me spoke of this over breakfast—we spoke very little, in fact. When we was done, Elmer went back out to the barn and I washed up the kitchen. Then I got a clean sheet from the cedar chest and cut out a tiny dress. I found a bit of blue ribbon and sewed it on the sleeves. And I fashioned a small white cap. When Elmer returned to warm up with coffee, I gave him my handiwork and the rest of the sheet. He blinked for a moment, and I said, For him, and you can line the coffin with what's left. That'll finish it off nice.

Then he looked at me straight on, for the first time that morning. I thank you, he said, and then he took them to the barn with him. After that, I kept going to the window, watching the tide when the snow'd stop. By afternoon, Elmer told me water was lapping in the stalls at the lower end of the barn, though it didn't seem to be rising real fast. He rubbed his hands by the fire and said, I'm going to bury him now.

I said, Don't you think you should wait till Mary comes to?

No, he said, they's no use waiting. What's in that box has got nothing to do with us now. I want it finished while we can.

He helped me get my coat on one more time. On the porch rail Elmer had left the box he'd half-made and half-found. Its planks were nailed shut and caulked tight with pine tar. Then he led back the holler and up the ridge a ways. He'd let the stock loose from the barn, and the cattle were circled under the cliff, around some hay he'd thrown them, and the horse was snuffing through the snow. We stopped where he'd shovelled a hole. It was already filling with water and snow. He swiped it out with his boot, then reached for the box and put it in the bottom. He heaved mud and ice down on top of it, then just stood and stared at the dirt. Snow collected on his hat and on top of his gloves. His face was streaked.

It seemed to me something should be said over the grave. Dear Jesus, Holy God, I said, closing my eyes, touching my gloves to them. Hear our prayer over this little child, for you are our refuge and strength, and a help in need. Therefore, we'll not fear, though the earth be gone, and the mountains be carried into the sea. There is a river———

No, Elmer cut in. We'll have none of that. I'll not start that now.

Lord have mercy on you, Elmer, I said drawing back, if you feel that way. I never felt so tired in my life. Or so cold. Elmer tamped around on the grave a final time, then took my arm and started toward the house. I thought I wasn't going to make it, I was limping so bad, but I did. My coat stunk of drowned wool and mud, and I spread it by the fire. I checked on Mary, then I slumped in the rocker and don't remember nothing else till Elmer shook me. At first I didn't know where I was. The room was almost dark, except for the fire. I put my hand to my face, and the grogginess started to pass. I asked if I'd been asleep long.

Pretty long, Elmer said. Mary's awake. I thought you should see.

I could hardly get out of the chair, my legs was so stiff, but Mary smiled when she saw me. She looked so thin and light that the quilts seemed to hold her down. Child, you're a welcome sight for these eyes of mine, I said. Can I get you some food?

She shook her head.

Elmer said, I give her some water, and she drank most. He ran his hand over her forehead, and touched the yellow hair glistening over the pillow. She smiled up at him, and her eyes closed.

No, Elmer said.

She's all right, I said. She's just got to sleep and heal herself. Elmer nodded. He looked like a dead man on his feet, sleep closing down his own face.

He brushed his eyes with his hands and said, Look, I'm going to stay here by the bed. You can have the one in the other room.

No, you go in there, I said, I've got some rest. Don't worry, I'll get you if Mary needs you.

He hesitated, then nodded. I think he must have been asleep before he hit the quilts. He'd never stopped, not even while I was asleep. The fire was burning strong and wood was piled by the hearth for the night. A fresh pail of water sat in the kitchen, and in the warming pan over the stove steamed corn bread, shuck beans, stewed tomatoes, and chunks of ham. Some coffee still in the pot. Before I ate, I stepped outside. I wanted the privy one more time before it was complete dark. But it was gone, and so was the smoke house. There was nothing but water, though it'd stopped snowing and raining both. I saw where Elmer had taken blankets and tied them through holes in the log walls and around the porch posts to anchor us. I thought, Lord have mercy. Surely he don't believe the tide'll get high enough to drift the house away. But it wasn't far from us, and had settled all around the barn. In such faint light, though, the water didn't seem to be moving at all—it looked more like soft fog hunkering down over the land.

I could hardly bend my legs, but I squatted off the end of the porch, then come inside and ate ever thing Elmer had left for me. The stewed tomatoes tasted so sweet and tart, I ate the rest of the jar. Yes, I ate and thought that's what we do—when Mary put up them tomatoes, she never guessed she might not eat them. No, we plan and think we take hold.

So I ate everything in sight, since I didn't know when I'd be eating again. And I didn't bother to clean up. I just went and sat by the fire. I tried to sleep but couldn't. I couldn't help but count out, one by one, my remedies and my cures. I'm a good midwife. I do what I can, and seldom for pay. When I bring a baby into the world, I like things washed and clean for it. In right weather, I go down by the chicken houses and gather catnip, then I make tea for both the mother and the baby. It brings the milk good in the mother's breast and it's the first thing the baby gets. I sweeten it a little and feed just a few drops at a time in a teaspoon. That cleans out the stomach and breaks out the hives. If the baby is fretful, twisting and rolling its eyes, the catnip tea will make it sleep.

I take sheets and pin a band around the baby so the navel will heal right, and pour castor oil over it to make sure. And if the baby gets galled, I reach up the chimney—a handful of soot rubbed in the sore place will heal it. And I keep the mother in bed at least two weeks. I even bring the chamber pot. I wait on her, and do everything to give a good start. I use the secrets and privacies of the woods—ironweed for a physic, sassafras for spring tonic, and boiled blackberry root for the summer complaint. So much, so much I know. And so much it don't make a difference. I could see that now.

I sat by the fire, it red and purple, deep and hot, and the dead crowded around me. I tried counting and recounting them away. Burvine tea for colds—I fed that to my niece to heal her affliction, but she drowned inside herself anyway. When I laid her out, her stomach just gurgled. And her dead with the consumption. She was still gurgling when we put her in the ground. Oh, to be laughed at and whispered around in death is a horrible thing. She warn't in this country long enough for people to remember anything else about her. Laurie was standing behind me now, her quiet, icy hand prickling the hair on my neck, and the fire snapped, like her insides did, even after she was dead. Why wouldn't her body let go? I guess the body does what it wants, with or without us. It will call back its blood or it won't.

And all we can do is stand by and say the words we've been taught will comfort us. We try and trust outside ourselves. And we do. But sometimes all fails—not even the preacher riding in gives grace. My mother rotted in her grave for eighteen years before she finally got her funeral. By then I'd said all the words. By then I knew them real well. She's crowding behind me too, crackling like the wood as it burns, her face black ash. She's shaking her head and clicking her tongue at the mess I've become—swole and bruised, and stuffed in men's clothes. And that little baby, and countless others, are all there too, pointing their tiny hands at me.

Somehow I must've dozed off. When I looked at the fire again, it was smoldering heavy. I heaved myself up and put a log on it. I picked up another and it was wet. I peered at the floor. A pool of smoke lay across the floor boards. But it wasn't smoke—water was slipping into the side of the room. I thought maybe I was still asleep, but when I put my hand down, it come back cold and dripping. I felt dizzy sick, and hurried to Elmer's door.

Elmer, I said, wake up.

I am awake, he said, immediate, like he'd never been asleep.

I said, The tide's in the house. Whatever on earth are we going to do. . . .

I heard him moving around, then he come out, looking more tired than before, the back of his hair sticking up where he'd been lying on it. I showed him the water. He looked at it without a word. Then he checked on Mary. He smoothed her hair and just stood by her. I sat back down by the fire. Finally, he come and set beside me. We didn't say nothing for what seemed like a long time.

At last he spoke. Maggie, you've done more for us than anybody in this world, you come when nobody else would have. I can't never find the words to say what it means.

I felt his hand on my arm. Then he said very low, There'll always be a place for you with us. You'll always be part of us.

My eyes started to burn again. Nobody had ever said such words to me, not even Luke. His hand tightened on me as he continued—And I think it best now you ready yourself. There's a way you can climb the cliffs over where the cattle was feeding yesterday. I'll give you the lantern and show you the way. It's steep, but I know you can make it.

I stared at him. He must have seen pain on my face.

He said again, I know you can do it. And he patted my arm. You might try for Sam Green's place, if they're not washed away. Or you might even get to Furnace Mountain, if the tide isn't so bad over there.

No, I said flatly, I'm not going.

He put his hand over mine. Now Maggie, he said, you'll do what I say. You know I'm right. I can't leave Mary, don't think she'd live, going over them cliffs, either across the horse if we could find her, or strapped to me. No, I'm going to stay put till they ain't a choice. But you should make ready. The water don't seem to be coming up quick, but if it should, I'll have to move fast.

I shook his hand away. I said, I may seem just old and in the way to you, but I ain't leaving. If you can wait, I can.

And I did. He couldn't budge me out of there. I told him I was more scared of them slick high cliffs than that sinking house, and besides, my legs weren't working—those made as good excuse as any, and finally he believed me. So Elmer kept the fire going as long as he could. By the time water swamped the hearth, it was daylight. I put as much dry tinder in the stove as I could to keep the chill off, and propped more logs around it to dry. Well, the water spread halfway across to Mary's bed, filled the back room, and then paused, as if watching and reconsidering. By afternoon it'd inched back a little, the sun come bleak through the clouds, and we'd lasted through what turned out to be the worst tide on Red River.

It was a couple of days before Luke and some of the others got through and told us. Then I heard my own house was wrecked. The kids weathered it all but our things were mostly ruined. In some ways, Elmer had been lucky. Not much in his house got hurt. The privy and smokehouse were gone, but his big barn had held, though mud covered its walls over six feet up. The hay in his loft was not touched, and most of his stock had wandered to higher ground. It turned out the big mare had found her way back to Sam Green's farm, but nothing was left there. The water come through so fast, the family'd just had time to get out. All their cattle and hogs was drowned. I guess Sam was extry glad he'd been generous and lent his horse to Elmer—that's all he had left.

As soon as Mary was stronger, Elmer come and helped with our place. He was as handy a man as ever lived on this river. When our floors dried and buckled and tore up, he got more boards and put in better than we'd had before. He brought us a milk cow and enough hay to see her through the winter. And ever time he went to the store, we knew it, even if we didn't see him. Always a box with flour and side meat and sugar would be left on the porch, stuff he never knew nothing about, he said. I believe he'd have given us most of what he had, if we'd let him. And that spring, after Luke came down bad with the consumption, he was there more. He even worked in the fields with our boys, though George was almost grown. He'd bring his boy, and he'd put my littlest ones on his knee and play with them like they was his own. And he wouldn't listen to taking a penny. No, I'd saved his Mary.

I can look at her now, sitting by the window, his sock twisted in her fingers, and know she is trying to force his live foot back into it. Or her boy's. Elmer and her son dead, no family left. She seems to me like she did on those awful nights of the tide. She never found her strength again. Her lips and cheeks shine glassy, like the stalks of wild touch-me-not that grows by the river and waves so gentle. It's like she never got all her blood back, and the light from the window goes through her skin like it would through a pool of water.

I turn from her to the bodies on the saw horses. I pull aside the sheets, and peel off the cool cloths I'd put over their heads. No, they haven't done no good. Elmer's face is starting to flatten, black and jellylike. But finally I do it. I tell him how I've loved him, and I give the kiss which is the hardest and the last and the only.

I can barely get outside. I get sick in the weeds by the porch. When I can breathe again and feel the ground biting into my knees, I wipe my face on my apron and steady myself. I try and sit on the steps. The sun has passed away down the river and sunk behind the ridges, but the sky brightens, streaming from nowhere and everywhere at once. I look down the holler, and it's like I'm seeing it for the first time, clear and strange and unknown. The trees seem thin, pared down to their trunks, sunlight warping through them. And then I see Elmer, standing over the grave of his lost boy, the one never his, and now I see what he saw then.

In a little while, John and Cora Wilkins walk along Gladie from the river. Cora follows John, her arm a quiver with a basket of fried chicken. The grease smell makes my throat close again, and I can't say hello in return. I hear them speak to Mary, slurpylike. Then they've hurried back on the porch, clenching their noses. I know without looking, hear their furious whispers.

He, sniffing and coughing—They're going to have to be poured in them coffins soon.

And she—John, I'm telling you, that stink and the way they was struck down, it's the Lord's judgment. It's the witness of the Lord and His curse.

I can't stand to hear it. I keep watching Elmer, his eyes so dark and fire-dirty against the snow and the flood. There is a river, I say again, and finish what was started that day—There is a river, and it flows where no man can see.

EPILOGUE

FROM RED RIVER
TO COON CREEK

Well, they took his hammer and they wrapped it in gold,
They gave it to Polly Ann,
The very last word John Henry ever said to her
Was Polly do the best you can. . . .
"John Henry"

In 1936, Lily May Ledford left the Red River Gorge to begin her career as a professional musician. She had been "discovered" by John Lair at a talent contest in Rockcastle County, Kentucky, and signed a five-year manager's contract with him. As music librarian at WLS in Chicago and a sharp promoter who handled talent on the side, Lair provided her with a chance to break into radio at the nation's top hillbilly station.

At that time, WLS was owned by the *Prarie Farmer*, which had a large distribution throughout the Midwest. *Stand By* magazine was printed on one floor of the station, and "The National Barn Dance," also known as the "NBC Alka Seltzer Hour," was staged at the station's Eighth Street theater. Though heavily publicizing its talent, the station exacted much in return from its performers. They were highly disciplined and expected to stay at work all day, and when not rehearsing or broadcasting, were encouraged to socialize in facilities provided for them. Quickly Lily May realized for the first time what it meant to be a full-time professional musician. Like many performers before her, she had learned her style of playing and stock of music from rural traditional sources, yet now she found herself having to please radio executives like John Lair, and their diverse listening audiences.

Lily May has recalled to me part of that reshaping process: "Mr. Lair found out I could play the banjo so he borrowed Scottie Wiseman's and said, 'Let's hear you pick.'

"I said, 'Mr. Lair, I'd rather fiddle. I just pick the old-timey way and no one wants to hear that.' Scottie played a little more modern style and I was kind of ashamed to play in front of him. I also had a real bad lisp. But at the time I could sing higher than a sparrow on a barn roof, or low, either one. So I sat down and picked 'John Henry' and it tickled Mr. Lair. As I sang a little crowd gathered around and cheered me on. And I begin thinking, 'All right. Maybe they accept this kind of playing.' And Mr. Lair said, 'You go on the banjo. From now on, the fiddle is just incidental.'

"I said, 'Mr. Lair, I ain't got no songs much, because my

daddy couldn't sing and I just know some old ballads Momma has. And I can't pick them on the banjo. They're slow.'

"He said, 'We'll start out on songs like "Sourwood Mountain" and then I'll write out some more old ones we've nearly forgotten and add a few words to them. We'll get you a lot of songs, because that banjo is what you'll make it on. We've got plenty of good fiddlers and you'll run into a good many more, but your style of banjo is scarce. In fact, I don't know of anybody in radio right now who's doing it.' He called it the *Tennessee Rap* or the *thumb-dropping style.* I never did call it anything but just picking the banjo and letting it go at that. Later I believe Pete Seeger named it *frail.* Now I never heard it called that before, but Pete Seeger done so much to promote banjo playing he deserves to call it what he wants."

During her stay at WLS, Lily May appeared on a variety of programs, including "The National Barn Dance." Another show, a local one sponsored by Pinex Cough Syrup, featured a square dance in play party format with Lily May and Chick Hurt among its performers, and was written by John Lair. Lily May also became part of the Pine Mountain Merry Makers, a group which included Red Foley.

However, despite her success, she remained at the station for only a year, because John Lair had other ambitions for himself and the performers he had under contract. What he envisioned was staging his own shows from a music complex to be built in his native Renfro Valley, Kentucky. With these plans in mind, he moved to Cincinnati, where he was closer to Renfro Valley and could supervise the construction, and he acquired broadcast time on radio stations throughout the Cincinnati area, including WLW, a 50,000 watt powerhouse, and WCKY, a 10,000 watt station then located in Covington.

He brought such performers with him from Chicago as Red Foley, Girls of the Golden West, and Slim Miller, and he put together several new acts, including the highly popular comedy team of A'nt Idy and Little Clifford. His most novel creation, however, was a string band consisting entirely of women performers. Lily May became leader of this group, and was joined by her sister, Charlotte, along with Evelyn Lang from Greenville, Ohio, and Esther Koehler from Wilton, Wisconsin. Although audiences at first were startled by the idea of an all-girl string band, especially one led by a woman banjo player who stood six feet tall, the Coon Creek Girls turned out to be an immediate success. Lily May remembers quite clearly when the band first came together:

"Since my sister's name was Rosa Charlotte and mine was Lily May, we decided to have flower names for all the girls. We named Esther, Violet; and Evelyn, Daisy. Now then, we said our theme is 'Flowers Blooming in the Wild Wood,' a popular song at the time and we changed the words a little to fit us:

There's a Lily that is blooming in the wild wood,
A Rose that is blooming there for you,
And the Violet's sweet with dew, and the lovely Daisy too,
We are flowers that are blooming there for you.

"So, all that went over all right, but when we decided to call ourselves the Wild Wood Flowers, Mr. Lair laughed and said, 'I think, girls, a name like the Coon Creek Girls is bound to let everybody know you are a country band and do only country music, and Coon Creek Girls just couldn't be better.'

"We said, 'Mr. Lair, there ain't no Coon Creek where any of us is from.' And he said, 'Oh well, that doesn't matter in the least. Your audience out in radio land don't know that.' So he named us, and the Coon Creek Girls we became.

"Finally, he auditioned us at WCKY Covington, and we took like a house afire the first week. Because we were the first all-girl string band on radio, we startled people. At the beginning they stared like they didn't believe and craned their necks, but by the time we got done, they tore the house down with applause. It was mostly the middle-aged and old people, farm people and the very, very poor that went for the Coon Creek Girls. When we'd go on the program each day—we had thirty minutes at noon—they would be lined up way down the block and round to the next just trying to crowd into the studio. And us girls got baskets of fan mail and cakes and homemade candy. We got flowers and crocheted little things, embroidered handkerchiefs with tatting, and marriage proposals.

Even some would bring a kettle of hot soup, wanting to come with us and help eat it. It was the Depression, you know. And babies were being named after us, and calves and pigs. We got so much attention, we got spoiled, I guess."

During this period in the late Thirties, rural families in the Ohio River Valley were gathering around their radios in ever-increasing numbers, as were those who migrated from Appalachia to northern industrial centers in search of jobs. To them, such groups as the Coon Creek Girls became household names.

In addition to studio work, the Coon Creek Girls began booking out in Ohio, Indiana, and Kentucky, often performing with A'nt Idy and Little Clifford, and with Whitey Ford, the "Duke of Paducah," who acted as their master of ceremonies. It was not uncommon for them to give seven or eight shows a day, at times racing through what Lily May describes as *bicycle dates*: "Two theaters close together would book us the same day and when a movie was showing at one, we'd run to the other and play, then have to run back again, although the towns could be several miles apart. We'd have to stay in costume from the time we got there at noon till midnight, and do five shows at each. We did a lot of that, and of course would have to get back to the station for our broadcasts the next day."

One of the high points of their career occurred in 1939, when they were invited to play at the White House during a visit by the king and queen of England. For this occasion, Eleanor Roosevelt planned a program showcasing different kinds of American music, and she chose such diverse performers at Kate Smith, Alan Lomax, Lawrence Tibbett, Marian Anderson, and a black church choir from the Washington, D.C. area. To represent hillbilly music, or what perhaps out of politeness was referred to as "Songs of the Ohio River Valley," Mrs. Roosevelt wanted the Coon Creek Girls. As a preview in the *New York Times* observed:

> But what probably attracted Mrs. Roosevelt is the quartet's vocal quality and natural gayety. They keep to the thin, unsentimental harmony of hillside hymn-singing;

the tripping patter of farmyard ditties, or the half-mocking, half-earnest balladry of a log fire, gourds on the wall, and hollows and ridges all around. Expatriate Kentuckians on farms or industries north of the Ohio River are homesick for this sort of thing, and no one gives it to them better than these girls who mean to be 'nachral' in the White House. (June 4, 1939, sec. 9, p. 6)

Lily May enjoys recalling just how "nachral," and how exciting, this experience was for them: "Mr. Lair said, 'Now, you're not to wear calico dresses. The committee is afraid it might be shocking to the queen. Wear street dresses, but don't wear spike heels—I can't stand for you to do that! If you are presented personally to their majesties, you'll have to curtsy.' He tried to show us how, and Mr. Lair was a short rotund man—he got tickled and we did too, but we made a stab at it.

"So the big night came to play in the East Ballroom. We were formally announced, and we ran out and lit into 'How Many Biscuits Can You Eat?' which had been a request of President Roosevelt's. About the first verse and chorus, I begin to look around. They were all four in the front row as close to me as my banjo over there. And we were pretty nervous because the people in charge of us were. Then I saw all the beautiful chandeliers and splendor, the stage bordered all the way round with ferns, these beautiful clothes on the elite of Washington, D.C.—there were eighty-nine guests besides the Roosevelts and the king and queen.

"And I begin to feel a little stage fright. It was pretty chilly, and not quite the same as playing the school house. On their faces was a different look than I was used to, a look of refinement and the kind of smiles that are—I don't know what you'd call them—rehearsed—and I begin to get worried we wouldn't go over with these people.

"We had been told to behave ourselves and not stare, but I kept catching them out of the corner of my eye. Roosevelt was just grinning as broad as any country boy, like he was having a good time. And Eleanor Roosevelt was a much better looking woman than I'd ever seen in any pictures. She had a pink chiffon dress on, but not fluffy. It was kind of slim and seemed to go with her coloring. Her skin looked nice, white and pink. And she smiled all the time and was friendly with everybody around her.

"The queen was smiling so beautifully too. She wasn't a glamorous looking woman, but she had a doll-like face and was pretty. Her gown was—now, it didn't look anything like rhinestones. It sparkled, but was muted, like water running over pebbles. And the beautiful tiara or whatever you call it that they wear on their head, she had that on. Well, she's not nearly as subdued as her daughter. No, she was more friendly looking and seemed easy to please.

"But the king had me worried because his face was absolutely a pure blank and I couldn't read anything in it. He had on all this military regalia, all those ribbons and pins and decorations. And he sat there just as straight as a ramrod, not moving a muscle in his face—he could have been dead and just propped up there! And I thought, 'Aw, he's not having any fun—he'd rather be in jail than be here.' And I wasn't liking him much.

"So we finished 'How Many Biscuits,' and later I got to thinking maybe he didn't like them—maybe he was a corn-bread man, you know! Well, our next song was 'Soldier and the Lady.' It's an English ballad and Mr. Lair thought that would be something for the king and queen. Sis and I sang it as a duet. The last one was 'Get Along Home, Cindy,' Roosevelt's favorite folk song. I swung around for one more look at the king sitting there stiff and deadpan, but saw him tapping his foot. And buddy, then I felt all right. I thought we had him just a little bit!"

Sometimes Lily May adds the following note to this story: "We had dressed in a little kind of library, and Sis had stuck her money under her garter—we used to wear garters and rolled our silk stockings around them. And that twenty dollar bill had got loose and crawled down her leg and just straightened out, just as straight as it could be the whole time we was out there! Maybe that's what the king was shocked about! We didn't know it till we got back and there was nothing we could do but laugh—and we have, many times."

After their White House performance, a New York agent arranged bookings for the group throughout the region, and at the Stanley Theater in Pittsburgh the Coon Creek Girls were featured with a dance team, a comedy team, and a twenty-five-minute play by Orson Welles called *The Green Goddess*. Lily May remembers that "we was on the road with a little show, and it was the year after he (Welles) scared the world to death with his broadcast about the world ending, that 'War of the Worlds.'

"Orson Welles was a person that—how shall I say it— almost intimidated you. He was so artistic, so great, or so, well, I don't know. There seemed to be no friendliness or warmth in him. I heard him bawl out his valet in a manner that scared me. After the first show, they had such a time getting his lighting and everything right that he decided to change the format a little bit and he called me to the dressing room. Scared me to death. I did not know what he could possibly want.

"He was very, very nice. He says, 'Now here's what I want you to do. Your act comes just before mine. Let the other girls get off stage after you've had your bows, then you come back and say: *Now then, I want to tell you folks that we're getting ready to darken the lights. So hold onto your pocketbooks and your hats because this next big act is coming out.*' That was just a warning they were going to completely darken the house for his act. He said, 'Then you pick up your skirts and run to beat hell!' It was a great big stage, you know, in this house. So I liked him after that very much, but I really didn't have much contact with him. We played there for a week, then we hit some other places like the Earl Theater back in Washington."

In the fall of 1939, John Lair completed his music complex at Renfro Valley. Demanding that every detail be authentic and old-fashioned, he built the barn and dining lodge with local stone and lumber, and the tourist cabins with log fireplaces, hand-made furniture, and pegged floors. As in the past, he took many of his regular performers with him, such as Slim Miller, Red Foley, Jerry Beherens, and A'nt Idy and Little Clifford. He also hired two new comedy teams: Little Eller and

Shorty Hobbs; and Homer and Jethro, who Lily May recalls "were about seventeen or eighteen and had been down in Knoxville *wild-catting*, working for nothing on stations in order to book out. They were great unusual comedy and polished musicians besides, and they encored at Renfro so many times you couldn't hardly get them off the stage to save your life."

Lair, however, even wanted most of his performers to be Kentuckian, a desire which was at least partly responsible for breaking up the original Coon Creek Girls.

"Daisy and Violet didn't want to come," Lily May has said. "Mr. Lair had always featured Sis and me more than them. Red River or Appalachian music wasn't all we played, but Mr. Lair had wanted to keep us typical of native Kentucky and didn't want anything that would show those two girls were from up North and Yankees. So they were kept in the background or at least not pushed for solos. I hated to lose them awful bad, but we had another little sister coming along." Fourteen-year-old Minnie Ledford was given the stage name of Black Eyed Susan, and the Coon Creek Girls became a Ledford sister string band.

Renfro Valley enjoyed great success, especially during the years around World War II. Its Saturday Night Barn Dance, for example, drew an audience of as many as 10,000 people for its weekend performances. Two shows were also picked up by the CBS radio network and aired over most of the United States. The better known of these was "The Sunday Morning Gathering," a program still being broadcast today.

"Now, we changed our style for a semi-religious show like that," Lily May recalls. "The sponsors, Ballard and Ballard Flour, and the network would not have tolerated banjo picking and old-timey stuff like we was doing on the stage Saturday night. No, we had to get other songs. Well, Mr. Lair had a vast music library there, one of the greatest collections in the country I've been told. He was offered $50,000 for it by Gene Autry when we first went to Renfro Valley, but nothing would part him from it. Well, none of us could read a note of music, so we would find old English ballads like 'Lord Bateman' and

'Lord Lovell' and there'd be several versions of them in those books. We'd take them to Jerry Beherens who could read music. He would sing each version and we'd see which one would make the best harmony, which we would have to work out, of course. Boy, us Coons kept busy because we had to have a new song every week. Most were in a minor key, which we had never sung in, but we learned. And I begin to get carried away with minor harmony. I stayed in that library all the time hunting songs and would bother Jerry to death to teach me the tunes. Then I'd teach them to Rosie and Black Eyed Susan and we'd put them on the air.

"We got to singing old populars like 'Far Away Places,' 'Sweet Summer's Gone Away' which was one of our best, 'Come, Birdie, Come,' and an old, old ballad called 'The Death in the Swamp.' At the beginning and end of the show we always sung a hymn and a church bell was rung. And we used 'Take me Back to Renfro Valley' for a theme—that was one of Mr. Lair's best songs, and I think it's pure poetry."

During the eighteen years they played at Renfro Valley, the Coon Creek Girls also booked out over a four or five state area and participated in a number of special performances. In 1943, for instance, Lily May took part in a one hour, live broadcast titled "The Martins and the Coys" (and billed as a "mountain ballad opera"), written by Elizabeth Lomax, arranged by Alan Lomax, and produced by English producer Roy Lockwood. Broadcast directly to Great Britain from New York over the BBC, this show also starred Burl Ives, Pete Seeger, Woody Guthrie, and Will Geer. Because of its success, another titled "The Old Chisolm Trail" was broadcast a few months later and included all three Coon Creek Girls.

As Lily May describes it, "'The Martins and Coys' was about two feuding families and how a Coy and a Martin fell in love and had to sneak about their courting. And there's a bear hunt and all in there. Then two boys who feuded at home wound up having to fight in the war and made friends in the trenches. Burl Ives and me done love songs like 'Little Turtle Dove' when a Martin and one of the Coy girls were meeting in the woods. When he had to go to the army, he'd sing, 'Oh, fair ye well, my little turtle dove,' and I'd answer back, 'Although you may go ten thousand miles away, you'll return to me, my love.' I was taking the part of the actress. The woman doing the speaking parts had a high-pitched voice and mine is a bit deep, and you could tell it wasn't her doing the singing! But that's the way it was. Any episode in the story was building up to a song. This was still during war time, and they set the broadcasts for when Pete Seeger was on leave.

"It was great working with these people. Instead of being hippy types, they were called bohemians and we'd go to their houses and just sit on the floor. They had rounds of cheese and you'd cut your own bread, everything was served roughly in the way of refreshments and beer. We played music and had conversation and that brought all the actors and the musicians together, and the producer and all the Lomaxes. We didn't have any partying at the studios. Boy, it was grueling rehearsals because the program had to go live. They couldn't perfect it and tape a little at a time like they do now, so we rehearsed until we were crazy. Then we would relax at somebody's apartment, usually in Greenwhich Village, and have a party, then get back to the grindstone the next morning.

"One day we had two great visits. Bess Lomax asked us out to breakfast and when we got there, she called Barney Josephson who owned Uptown Cafe Society and Downtown Cafe Society. At that time Burl Ives was playing late shows in both these clubs. He was also on Broadway in a play and was the big money earner on our show—actually he was the only one who was a coming star or already there. Bess called this Mr. Josephson and told him about us girls. She said, 'They're extremely pretty and highly talented' and she told about the king and queen performance. So he got interested, as we later found out.

"Then we went from Bessie's to Woody Guthrie's near Coney Island. His place was a four-room apartment in an old house, and he'd married a ballet dancer and had a child. We ate lunch, and again it was the long hard rolls with great hunks of Polish sausage between them and boiled corn on the cob. Their furniture was rustic and collected odds and ends, things from Mexico and other countries and artistic looking because he had an artistic wife. Anyway, after lunch we went to the beach, hunted for shells and waded in the water.

"The next night after that relaxing, we did our broadcast. There were only two fluffs on the entire show and Woody caught both of them, I believe. He had a singing and a speaking part, and he fumbled with the script. He was sick then, you could tell. Skinny and yellow and dried up— Momma'd have said, 'There goes the sorriest thing that ever was,' if she would have seen him pass the house. His hair needed cutting and he needed a shave most of the time, and he talked real country. He was from Oklahoma. When we had to go from one studio to another, Woody'd walk down Broadway elbowing his way through the crowd, singing and picking his guitar. Sometimes he'd sling it across his back—he never would take a case because he was liable to want to play anywhere. We'd get on the subway and if the car was kind of empty, he'd go off in a corner and sing 'Little Birdie' or something like that. Sometimes he'd sit in a deep study and look lonely, like he wanted to isolate himself from other people. At other times he was sociable. People who knew him said he was bitter, and he was the one who began writing some protest stuff, I believe.

"When the show was finally over, everybody hugged everybody, and Bess began making calls to others who had helped in the background. After we did 'The Old Chisolm Trail' in the fall and had gone back home, the offer came from the Cafe Society. Mr. Josephson wanted a six-month contract and for us to alternate between the two clubs. The pay was great and at first Sis and Minnie agreed to try it. Minnie wasn't married and could go. I was free and at the time wasn't under contract with John Lair, so I felt I could. But Sis had two little children and at the last moment backed out and we had to tell him no, after we'd already accepted.

"Well anyway, before that happened, Woody wrote me and said, 'Gee, I hear you're coming to the big city.' And he begin talking like he was pleased at the prospect of seeing us again and about what fun we'd had doing the shows. Then he started about the day we went to the beach and about the mussel shells—how some were pearly, pink, and polished on the inside, and smooth and beautiful on the outside. And yet, you'd notice that some were lacerated and scaly, and their inside color was grayish and dull. Some were ripped almost in two, yet they'd all come through the same storms, pushing the same obstacles and so forth. 'And it's amazing,' he said, 'that some came out so polished and so beautiful to look at and touch, and others came out so torn. Yet they'd all been through the same.'

"I couldn't understand why he wrote so long about those shells and was beginning to think he was a fool, but Minnie had a sharp mind and said, 'No, he's speaking of us, how coming to the city might change us. It's advice in a way.' Those Uptown and Downtown Cafe Societies were stepping stones to Hollywood and other places and if we went higher, Woody knew the fights and temptations we would go through. And his advice was talking about these shells, likening us to them, warning us to be careful and stay as we were—clean. Or we could come out ruined, drunkards or on dope or something. I'm sure that's what he meant. But we didn't go. So I never saw Woody again, and it was not long until he was in and out of the hospital with Huntington's disease—for fifteen years, I think it was."

In 1955, the Coon Creek Girls briefly appeared on Broadway in a show titled "The Old Dominion Barn Dance." Headed by Sunshine Sue, this show also included Earl Scruggs, Lester Flatt, and the Foggy Mountain Boys. "Broadway," Lily May remembers, "was like places we'd always played. Yet Red Skelton came to the first night and so did Joan Blondell. They had a bag of popcorn and just enjoyed the show. Of course all the critics were there too, and Walter Kerr was the one that ripped up our Elizabethan ballad, 'Gone Away.' He said, 'These girls, they're fugitives from the Borscht-Belt.' That's a section of little old theaters which featured scab acts and was full of burlesquey comedians more hideous than they were funny. I've heard it was called the Borscht-Belt because many of the entertainers were from the Balkans and that's where most of their audience was from, so they had a certain crowd that kept those places open.

"And Kerr said we weren't from Kentucky, weren't mountain women—we was all put on. And Mr. Lair got so mad. He wrote a letter and showed us a copy when we got home. And he said, 'What do you mean? They lived here at so-and-so time, on a certain date.' He wrote like a critic. Then he summed it all up: 'Broadway isn't nothing but a big carnival anyhow.' And it was.

"It was like an over-sized fair with little booths that sold pornography and everything in this world. And those theaters where the plays went on weren't elaborate looking on the outside, at least the ones I saw. Well, anyway, one critic named John Chapman, said, 'The Coon Creek Girls are quaint. It's not my kind of music, but I still say it was well presented.' Then some said the whole show was good. Earl Scruggs and them didn't get as much coverage as I expected, but they weren't criticized either. Some critics razzed Sue more than anybody. She sung ballads sweet, like a little girl. She was pretty, though, and photogenic, but her speaking to the audience was over-sweet, like talking sweetly down to children. Years later I saw her on TV doing a commercial with Karo syrup!"

By 1957 when the Coon Creek Girls retired as a group, the popularity of their type of music had declined, and live radio programs featuring performers like themselves had virtually vanished from the air. With the rise of Nashville as a major recording center, the overwhelming popularity of rock and roll, the widespread use of electrical instruments, and the impact of television, old-time music like theirs almost disappeared. As Lily May has put it, "our fans disappeared and went over to modern country music, and we just had a few loyals who came around and wrote us. We stopped drawing crowds, though Mr. Lair kept trying and sending us out. So we quit and joined the PTA and Red Cross, the Eastern Star and things of that nature, just became housewives and mothers and let the music go."

However, the rise of the so-called urban folk movement in the early 1960s generated a revival of interest in earlier traditional styles, including old-time string band music, and in 1967, Ralph Rinzler, a leading authority on old-time music, convinced the Coon Creek Girls to come out of retirement and play at the Newport Folk Festival in Rhode Island. This turned out to be a new start for the band, playing before a new type of audience.

"College kids never came to see Renfro Valley," Lily May has said, "and when we played out, if I saw a group of them coming down the street, me and my calico costume would cross to the other side because invariably one would say something and the rest would laugh. So when we played that festival and the audience was all these young people I thought, 'Oh, what'll they do to us!' Why, they ate up everything we did and that was a great thrill for us. I saw old-time music was not done with some of them."

In recent years, Lily May has continued her career, booking out as a solo act at festivals and on extensive tours. She also received a National Endowment for the Arts Grant in 1979 which enabled her to give banjo and fiddle workshops at Berea College and other schools in Kentucky. She's added story telling to her playing and singing, a combination that suggests the older traditions of the minstrel show and the vaudeville stage, and demonstrates her great presence and versatility as a performer.

"I think," she says of her playing, "I was just one of the few younger ones to take up frail picking because my daddy picked it, my granddaddy picked it, and some of my uncles who were old men when I was a little girl picked that way. Even when I was playing at WLS in the 1930s, my music was the most old-fashioned there and of course I got teased a lot. As I've told you there were several Kentuckians at WLS, but their music was more up to date. It was still called hillbilly, but it wasn't as hillbilly as mine.

"Now there are jillions of kids picking it up everywhere I go, and they're doing a much better and fancier job than us old ones did. But it still can be called old-timey like ours. So old-time music is being revived, and I think it may be long lasting. I thank goodness for it, because if it had been let go another twenty years, I'm afraid it would've been lost all together.

"It's been people like Mike Seeger and John Ullman, Ralph Rinzler, and Loyal Jones down at Berea who have been so enthusiastic and helped me get back to playing. Now with all the workshops and performances, it's almost more than I can get to, but it's wonderful. It's our old-time music people seem hungry for, and anything I can tell them about myself and my way of life, my music or my father's—they crane their necks and their eyes get big to hear it. And it gives me a feeling of accomplishing something I never thought I could."

As John Lair has told me about Lily May and the Coon Creek Girls, "They were absolutely original and authentic; they were the real thing." And certainly, Lily May deserves mention as part of the history and development of American country music: not only as leader of the first all-girl string band on radio, but as a woman who has continued to pass on the rich musical heritage she learned as a child in the Red River Gorge of eastern Kentucky and has preserved over the years.